PRAISE FOR
THE PERPETUAL SUMMER

"Chuck's sharp, wry insights into the absurdity of the corporate world reveal his existential need for more meaning in his life, and many scenes are genuinely funny...Phillips's clever blend of the absurd and the serious will have readers looking forward to Chuck's next adventure."

— *Publishers Weekly*

"This one's all about style, and the juicy bits are all in the evocative writing—'the wonderfully sad pink of an early Sunday morning'—and the offbeat information: to see in darkness, look out the corner of your eye."

— *Booklist*

"In this darkly humorous crime novel, Phillips nicely contrasts Chuck's action-packed sleuthing with his humdrum corporate battles. This atmospheric mystery vividly captures a diverse, contemporary Los Angeles that will still be recognizable to readers of Raymond Chandler."

— *Library Journal*

"Nuanced character portraits and slowly building suspense make this both an involving human story and a crackling crime yarn."

— *Kirkus Reviews*

THE BIG CON

A CHUCK RESTIC MYSTERY

Adam Walker Phillips

PROSPECT
·PARK·
BOOKS

Published by Prospect Park Books
2359 Lincoln Avenue
Altadena, California 91001
www.prospectparkbooks.com

Distributed by Consortium Book Sales & Distribution

Library of Congress Cataloging-in-Publication Data

Names: Phillips, Adam Walker, 1971- author.
Title: The big con / Adam Walker Phillips.
Description: Altadena, California : Prospect Park Books, [2018] |
Series: A Chuck Restic mystery
Identifiers: LCCN 2017051544 (print) | LCCN 2017055777 (ebook) |
ISBN 9781945551277 (Ebook) | ISBN 9781945551260 (softcover)
Subjects: LCSH: Murder--Investigation--Fiction. | Private investigators--
Fiction. | GSAFD: Mystery fiction.
Classification: LCC PS3616.H4475 (ebook) | LCC PS3616.H4475 B54
2018 (print) | DDC 813/.6--dc23
LC record available at https://lccn.loc.gov/2017051544

Cover design by Nancy Nimoy
Book layout and design by Amy Inouye, Future Studio
Printed in the United States of America

For Scott

A FIASCO OF MY OWN DOING

My firm paid them upward of a million dollars each year to spout nonsense, but everyone agreed it was money well spent.

Power of One® was both a misleading and accurate name, for the company consisted of two full-time employees—but only one who really mattered. Like most leadership consulting firms, they were centered around a single personality. Any additional employees were really only there to serve as vessels for the founder's wisdom. After years of spewing someone else's thoughts, the people working in such a place tended to shed their employee status and take up the mantle of the acolyte, and the founder attained near mythical status.

Julie St. Jean relished that.

Like many people who command a room, Julie actually spoke very little. Her business partner, Rebecca, did all the talking, but Julie was the only one you heard. She would quietly survey the training sessions from somewhere off to the side of the room, most often with a cup of tree-bark tea that she studied with the determination of one of the world's great thinkers unraveling one of the world's great issues. At some point in the session she would politely ask Rebecca if she could add to the discussion. She wouldn't come to the front of the room. Instead, she'd remain in some hard-to-see place and wait while those in attendance turned and craned their necks in her direction. She would begin in a faint whisper, the intended result being that everyone in the room was forced to lean in to catch what she had to say. What came out was often a masterful display of subterfuge.

"Sometimes," she'd begin haltingly, "the hardest decisions in life are the ones you don't actually make."

Everyone in the room would collectively nod their heads as one might after hearing something truly profound. And if you somehow missed it, lead instructor Rebecca would let a few moments of silence hang out there to allow Julie's words to fully sink in before returning to the session. It was too often the longest five seconds of my life.

"Food for your brains," Julie would finish with a shrug, appearing almost embarrassed to have spoken in the first place. "Do with it what you will, if anything."

The false humility was lost on everyone. They gobbled it up. No one ever took the next step and actually reflect on the words long enough to realize that everything she said was gibberish.

Her personal branding helped sell it. She had a mesmerizing mane of silver hair that transformed her plain, gray eyes into something bright and lively. She sported a uniform of sorts that consisted of oversized, white button-down shirts with the sleeves rolled up and flowing black pants. In combination, the ensemble took on an Eastern flair like that of a progressive karate sensei, one who could unleash a silent, roundhouse kick to the face at any moment. That potential threat was further enhanced by the fact that she had an unnaturally deep voice—deeper even than many men. I remember her first exchange with my old friend Easy Mike.

"I'm Julie," she said in her usual baritone.

"Bullshit you are!" said Easy Mike, but sensing yet another HR sit-down in my office, he quickly recovered. "No one this young," he said like a dutiful supplicant, "could speak with such wisdom."

Easy Mike was right about that aspect. Julie St. Jean still had a striking youthfulness, despite her advanced middle age. It was hard to tell how old she actually was, but I had personally known her for twenty-plus years. And in that time I had grown to respect her—albeit begrudgingly—if for no other reason than for her absolute mastery of our company.

Julie St. Jean's multi-decade-long campaign to land (and hold) the contract with my firm was executed with a strategy straight out of a missing chapter of Sun Tzu's *The Art of War*. She realized early on that while executive coaching could be a lucrative venture, it required a constant pipeline of fresh, insecure executives to keep the coffers full. You could make a living off of it but the opportunity was limited. To make the leap into the big money you had two choices: package your stuff into a series of seminars and books (a very tough proposition that typically led to more failures than successes) or bring your program not just to the executives of the firm but to the entire firm itself.

To take on a herd the size of our corporation, common sense would say you should start with the weak and sick trailing in the back of the group, the easy prey. Make your foothold there, use them to spread the word, and then steadily make your way up the ranks. But common sense would steer you wrong, because there are no grassroots movements in a corporation. Everything is top-down. What Julie St. Jean realized was that she needed to take down the biggest bull in the herd in order to own the herd.

That bull was my boss, Pat Faber.

I've always felt that salesmen were the easiest pigeons, and as such, con men made the easiest marks. The ones who can spin a tale are the ones most susceptible to someone else's. Pat Faber was an obvious choice. His career path somewhat paralleled that of Julie St. Jean. In many ways, they grew up together. Undeserved confidence and homespun aphorisms garnered Pat a reputation as a no-nonsense problem-solver. He rode that image to a level at the firm that got him an office with a mountain view through a three-paneled window.

The pyramid scheme worked its way down to my level about seven years ago. Everyone agreed that the entire company—not just the executives—could benefit from the wisdom of Julie St. Jean and Power of One, but it just wasn't feasible for those two individuals to teach all four thousand employees. What if, came the retort, we could "empower" a few associates at the firm to do the teaching for us (and pay a per-student fee back to Power of One)? My name inexplicably came up as the person to coordinate all of it. This afforded me a front-row seat to a brilliant display of corporate survival.

Julie St. Jean was many things, but mostly she was someone who ferociously fought for—and maintained—relevance. Her secrets were having her finger on the pulse of what people wanted and the ability to continuously reinvent herself.

She made her mark in the 1980s, during the testosterone-filled, greed-is-good period in Corporate America. She offered a no-bullshit tract that made it easier for executives to act like pigs when their coach, a woman no less, told them to. She threw out the "straight talk" schtick once the recession hit in the 1990s and CEOs were publicly a little more contrite and shamed by their excesses. That's when she began one of her Zen programs. The internet age launched a series of Innovate | Ideate | Invigorate seminars, and the most recent period was dominated by Socially Responsible Leadership, some vague, positive-sounding message to help justify ever-escalating executive-compensation levels.

Two weeks ago, the nonsense came to a crashing halt.

After twenty-five years of inanity, Power of One finally took that bold step into fiasco. The cruel truth that haunts every consultant business is that the dog-and-pony show works until it doesn't work anymore. I didn't relish what was to be their eventual replacement for another consulting firm with a different, shiny bauble but I didn't have much sympathy, either. They had made millions from us for many years and, as far as anyone could tell, had accomplished nothing.

The dismantling of Power of One was, in typical corporate fashion, a multi-year effort. They were never outright fired but rather were slowly starved to death. We gradually weaned ourselves off their programs until they reached a point where the caloric intake was no longer sustainable.

As if sensing the end was near, Julie St. Jean rallied for one last reinvention, or, as I imagined it, a death throe. The new program was a bit of a mélange of all their programs with a few new ideas thrown in. It reeked of desperation.

They added a third member to the act, a caricaturist, or, as she was introduced to me, a "Visioning Artist." For a time I thought she was a mute because she said nothing. She wore her hair long, a blond, frizzy mess that descended the entire length of her back. During brainstorming sessions she skipped around the room like a maiden at the Renaissance Faire, only her instrument wasn't a lute but a giant sketchpad. With a wedge of charcoal she captured the "essence" of the discussions in manically rendered mood drawings. She cranked these things out, tearing them from the pad and letting them fall to the floor as she moved on to the next rendering.

By the end of the session, the room looked like a bomb had gone off.

One jokester with a track record of inappropriate behavior enthusiastically participated in a brainstorm on what makes a healthy ecosystem. He rattled off responses like a leadership coach with the hiccups:

"Ramrod-straight ethics...

"A hard-line on discipline...

"A consistent thrust..."

Only when he used the word "girth" did I realize what he was doing. We spent the better part of the day walking on thinly veiled sketches of erect penises.

That's when Pat Faber dropped in. The semi-pornographic drawings crunched under his loafers as he made his way to the center of the room, where he slowly surveyed the scene with his hands on his hips. He picked up a white theater mask we had been using to help develop full-body expressions. He looked disgusted.

"Supposed to, um, 'uninhibit' us so we can communicate more clearly together," I sheepishly explained. Even their biggest disciple couldn't defend this one, and it showed on his face. "Listen, Pat, we need to talk about this," I began, trying to ease into the difficult discussion about breaking protocol and just killing his darling in one swoop.

"Yes, we do," he replied in a defeated voice.

I was overcome with an odd feeling of sadness for the old man. He was universally regarded as a buffoon and this spectacle was further proof of that, but I still felt a little remorse in having to deliver the message.

"Well, we gave it a good effort," I consoled.

"Maybe," he answered cryptically. Pat held up the white mask like it was a weapon. "I hope you can show some tangible results from this program of yours," he warned, and let the mask slip from his fingers.

I processed his words as the white face settled on the floor and stared blankly back up at me.

"Management committee meets on Monday next week," he said. "Come prepared to give an update."

I watched him leave, feeling the mixture of frustration and admiration normally reserved for the end of a magic trick. As your card is miraculously pulled from the performer's pocket, you admire his cleverness and equally despise him for tricking you.

Somewhere along the way, and I wasn't really sure when, I had landed on the hook for this debacle. And what had been a fiasco that I could once watch as a spectator from the shore now threatened to bring me down with the ship.

THE DOJO

All my years on the job had taught me there was no way to maneuver out of this. Once my name was on it, I owned it. I could remind everyone that I never believed in Power of One, that I was very vocal in expressing those views, and that I could even summon a catalogue of emails—tangible proof—that early on I recommended eradicating this scourge Pat Faber had unleashed on the firm. But all of that would go unheeded. Not only would nothing change but expressing those views publicly would be perceived as a further blemish on my record.

I could anticipate the response: "Chuck, let's not play the blame game." No one wanted to hear a recrimination, even if it had merit. "We need to focus on the now, and what you are doing to right this ship."

Never was I more engaged in my work than when it was threatened to be taken away. Fear proved, once again, man's greatest motivator. This coaching guru might be in the twilight of her career, but she wasn't going to take me down with her.

I had my assistant cancel all meetings for the rest of the week and schedule several all-day sessions with Julie St. Jean. I also dropped in on a couple of management committee members to give them a quick preview of Monday's presentation so they'd feel like they were in the know. And for the first time since I took this job some twenty years ago, I actually had to work on a weekend so we could rehearse exactly how to position Power of One's disastrous program as a ringing success.

The drive over to Julie's house was interminable not because there was traffic but because early on a Sunday morning there weren't any cars at all, just empty stretches of five-lane freeways that seemed to go on forever. I traveled at an unusually high speed through gray fog that filled the Los Angeles basin and obscured any view beyond a few hundred feet, making me feel like I was moving backward.

Palos Verdes Peninsula was a tony outcropping specifically designed to be very difficult to enter and even harder to leave. All major roads leading to it either funneled you to the massive port to the south or to the beach cities to the north. To actually penetrate the peninsula, you were routed through a series of roads laid out in concentric circles, whose intended effect was to make you feel like you were being herded by an overriding force.

At the core of PV was the incorporated town of Palos

Verdes Estates, one of the most heavily patrolled areas in the country, with a law enforcement–to–resident ratio that the International Union of Police Associations held as their high-water mark, plus some.

Julie's house was low and deceptively large. A layer of fog hugging the hilltop somewhat veiled the true extent of the wings protruding from each side of the main entrance. The outline of the house ran in a long, jagged line that traced the contour of the cliff, which I assumed was to maximize the ocean vistas from every room, even the coat closet.

I stared up at the moving clouds and the fine mist they deposited on everything below. We were officially in El Niño season but the serious rains had yet to begin. Ever-hopeful, I wondered just how close to the unstable cliff's edge this house might be as I made my way up to the entrance.

Two heavy doors were framed by panels of glass that gave a glimpse into the foyer. I tried the bell a few times and then an elaborate door knocker but got no response to either. Cupping my hands over the glass, I saw dark, empty rooms and then nothing as my breath's condensation obscured everything. I heard tires on the gravel behind me.

A black Town Car appeared from the pine grove shadows and came up the driveway. Rebecca emerged from one of the rear doors. I waited for Julie St. Jean to step out, always the last one to arrive on the scene for maximum dramatic effect. I learned early on that she applied her showmanship to all facets of life, including the order of who came through the door last. But no one trailed Rebecca out of the sedan.

"Sorry I'm late," she said. "Have you been waiting long?"

"No, I just got here," I answered, and watched the sedan back out of the driveway. "Where's the boss?"

Rebecca sensed my impending frustration.

"She'll be here," she replied firmly. "Let's go inside."

Rebecca pulled a key from her purse and with some effort swung the big door open. She hurried over to the alarm panel but stopped a few feet short. There was no chirping that signified a code was needed. She stared quizzically at the little box and then made an obvious statement.

"She must be here already."

"I rang the bell but didn't get an answer," I said, following Rebecca past a formal sitting room and into an expansive kitchen that looked like something out of a magazine photo shoot. Even the appliances seemed like decorations.

I was drawn to the westward-facing wall, which was really more of a window than a wall. It ran floor to ceiling, and on closer inspection, I could see hinges in the frame that meant the windows could fold open like an accordion door. Each of these probably cost twenty-five grand, and the entire west wall was covered in them. That, more than any other ridiculously expensive feature in the house, filled me with envy.

"Too bad it's cloudy," Rebecca said from the entrance to a hallway. "It's an amazing view from Long

Beach Harbor all the way up to Malibu."

But all I saw was a dense mist that shifted slightly in the onshore winds and made me slightly queasy as my eyes searched for something to fix on. I suddenly felt very cold and glanced around the room. They either didn't believe in heat or the system was out of order, because the house held the kind of cold that seemed to permeate every object inside it. The expensive terrazzo floors were probably pleasant in the heat of summer but on a wintry day like today you wanted something soft—a heavy pile rug, a threadbare throw, a scattering of hay, anything to keep the cold from coming up through the soles of your shoes.

Rebecca gestured for me to follow her. She led me down a long hallway lined with the same accordion doors as the other rooms. With no view to provide a distraction, it felt more like a dimly lit tunnel.

I followed a few feet behind Rebecca and found myself studying her figure. She had always been a slender woman but up close she looked even thinner. She wore black slacks that were always two sizes too large. Her belt, already cinching a narrow waist, looked like it could tighten to yet another hole or two.

I felt a little ashamed that I had known this woman for nearly twenty years and had only now taken the time to actually regard her with even the slightest interest. Julie's gravitational pull was just too strong, I thought. When you see Jupiter, who thinks to gaze at the nameless moons orbiting it?

The hallway banked away from the ocean and now

there were rooms on each side of us. Rebecca humbly pointed out her office on the left—half the size of Julie's on the opposite side and lacking the key feature of the house: any kind of view. We passed through a set of doors and entered the far southern wing. The décor changed dramatically from a pale, seaside color palette to something much more exotic.

It looked like a smorgasbord of Buddhist, Hindu, Babylonian, Turkish, and whatever other living and dead cultures and religions sat under the very wide umbrella category of "the East." Museum-quality artifacts lined the walls, and looming statuary stood guard in the corners. You could almost see the fingerprints of the looters who had "rescued" these antiquities from their tombs. Someone had overdone it on the frankincense air freshener, because it reeked of resin and made it difficult to breathe.

Rebecca stood proudly off to the side to let me take it all in. I had entered what executives far above my pay grade referred to as "the Dojo." This was where Power of One held its individualized coaching to work out specific challenges. These sessions were legendary among the C-suite members for their three-day antics and vows of secrecy regarding what went on. Over the years scraps had leaked out and rumors built them into an entire narrative that was probably only partly true. It was all part of the gimmick to make them "exclusive." And as obvious as it was, I still resented that I had never been asked to participate. I was deemed worthy enough to teach their nonsense to the masses at the firm, but I didn't warrant an invite into this sacred room.

And it pissed me off.

The annoyance that had been bubbling in me all morning was about to boil to the surface. I was annoyed that I had to work on the weekend, annoyed that I had to do so on the other side of the city on a cold Sunday, and annoyed that the person who put me in this situation didn't feel it necessary to grace us with her presence.

Rebecca unlatched the carved wooden doors to the official part of the Dojo. Beside the entrance was a stand holding a ceremonial rin gong singing bowl. I took up the mallet and struck the bell hard, too hard, and announced an entrance worthy of royalty.

"Entering!" I shouted.

Rebecca shot me a look that chastened me enough to regret the childish outburst. I grabbed the bowl in an attempt to silence it but the vibrations only made my hand numb and the bell continued its sickly tone.

Rebecca's glare went from me to an object in the dimly lit room. She took one step forward then two steps back. I entered the small room, which was covered in stone and sparsely decorated with a few low benches. At the center was another found object of some supposed religious significance, but on closer inspection I realized this one wasn't very ancient at all.

Her body was curled up like that of an exhausted child, her thumb extended toward her mouth where, if no one was watching, she'd find the soothing comfort to lull herself to sleep. Her head was cast in a halo of crimson, her long, blond hair now caught up in a matted mess in the sticky puddle.

I stared at the blood and my breath seemed to escape me. I found myself on one knee in a pose of exaggerated genuflection. I placed two fingers onto the cold stone, solemnly bowed my head, and vomited all over the floor.

JARGONITES

P alos Verdes Estates police officers buzzed in and out of the front door to the house in an endless stream. I didn't understand why so many uniformed officers were needed at an already-secured crime scene. The majority of them just stood around talking about last night's game. Of the handful of groups, only one discussed the actual murder.

They were led around by a young man in a new suit, the only one among them not in a uniform. I gathered he was new to the detective ranks by the way his peers followed him with begrudging respect and by the fact that he was relegated to perimeter duty when the real action was some hundred feet away in the Dojo. That didn't stop him, however, from forming a hypothesis about the killer.

"The perpetrator likely knew, or was very close to, the victim," he stated, and got a lot of head-nodding from the officers around him. Group-think led them to view whatever the young detective said as gospel. "Faced with the consequences of his actions," he continued, "disgusted with what he'd done to someone he was close to, he lost control of his bodily functions."

Unfortunately, the basis for this theory rested entirely on the fact that someone had thrown up at the crime scene. He incorrectly assumed it belonged to the murderer, not the guy sitting in a wingback chair ten feet from them.

"Actually, that was me," I said sheepishly. The nodding stopped and all eyes shifted in my direction. "I think it might have been—" I started, and then thought better of trying to explain it away on a stomach bug that was supposedly going around.

The police officers stared at me with the kind of pity reserved for a half-a-man. The young detective was less compassionate since I'd blasted a truck-size hole in his theory. He slowly made his way toward me.

"What's your connection to the deceased?" he asked.

I used to think jargon was a scourge unique to the corporate world but later realized it was the weapon of choice for every incompetent in every job in existence. The words themselves might be different, but the intent behind them was always the same—use a made-up language to make it sound like you know what you're talking about. Cops were some of the worst perpetrators.

"The 'deceased' has a name," I began, rising out of the chair to give my self-righteousness a little more weight. "Her friends know her by that name. The people who brought her into this world gave her that name."

The truth was I didn't know her name either. We must have been introduced at some point but she was always "that woman with the sketchpad" to me. All that, however, wasn't going to stop me from getting up on my cross in front of an insensitive cop.

"She may be just an object to you, young man, but she's still a human being to all of us."

The detective lowered his head like a contrite teenage boy. The other cops stared at their shoes. There was a fair amount of feet shuffling, and radios were turned down to bring a little more respectful quiet to the room.

"I'm sorry," the young detective finally said. "What was your friend's name?"

"That's hardly important right now," I stammered. "I knew her on a professional level. We were collaborators on a number of large initiatives at my firm. She was a creative dynamo, a real visionary, and a consummate team member. It's...it's tragic."

"Lois," said a voice behind me. "Her name is Lois."

Rebecca emerged from the hallway with the senior detective in tow. She entered the circle of police and gave the unfortunate woman the respect she deserved.

Lois Hearns was married, Rebecca related, didn't have any children, and lived in Burbank with her husband. She had worked for Power of One for nearly three years on a contract basis. She might have been raised in the Midwest but Rebecca couldn't be sure. She was an artist.

"Was Ms. Hearns working with you recently?" asked

the young detective.

Before Rebecca could answer, the lead detective stepped in. To prove he was in charge, he asked the same question, just in different words.

"She had a small role in one of our new engagement programs," Rebecca said.

"Can you think of a reason why she would be inside your house?" the older man asked.

Clearly the detective knew something I hadn't: that Julie St. Jean's sprawling Palos Verdes complex was where Rebecca lived as well as worked.

"I don't know," Rebecca replied.

"Does she have access to your home? Perhaps a key?"

"I've never given her a key," she answered.

The young detective chimed in that there was no sign of forced entry, but everyone, including Rebecca, ignored him.

"But that doesn't mean she didn't have one," Rebecca clarified.

There was a subtext to the latter part of her statement, something the lead detective quickly picked up on.

"When's the last time you spoke to your wife?" he asked.

Everyone at work naturally assumed that Julie St. Jean was a lesbian because of the "irrefutable" evidence of a deep voice, butch haircut, and androgynous clothing. But I don't think anyone had made the connection between Julie and Rebecca. I certainly hadn't.

Yet again, I took a moment to study Rebecca. For

twenty years I looked over this woman's shoulder when she spoke. We must have had countless conversations but not a single one that I could recall. I may have given her my physical time—often more than I gave to friends or relatives—but never a minute of my attention.

"Two days ago," Rebecca answered after a slight hesitation.

"And where was that?"

"We spoke on the phone."

"When's the last time you saw her in person?" the detective pressed.

"Almost a week," she whispered.

The lead detective glanced at his counterpart and made a subtle gesture in my direction. The young detective picked up on it and asked me to join him in the living room so he could ask me a few questions.

Curiosity aside, I was grateful not to have to witness the emotional undressing of a woman in front of a group of strangers. Rebecca was being forced to divulge the details of her relationship and all its ugly imperfections to people who didn't even know her. I didn't want to be one of them.

The young detective asked me a few meaningless questions and then drifted off to something more important. I lingered by the open front door. It felt like twilight but I knew it was much earlier. I found myself staring out through the trees toward the hypnotic lights of local news crews blinking on and off with each broadcast back to the studio.

"Sir," said a voice, "would you mind giving Ms. Piken

a ride to a hotel?" Rebecca stood next to the young detective. They both looked tired.

"If it's on your way…" Rebecca began. "All these years in LA and I never got a license. I might be the only one," she said to no one in particular.

"Of course," I answered, stirring myself back to the present. I must have been standing in the cold air for some time because my hands and legs were stiff. "Do you have a bag?" I asked.

"No," she answered quickly.

I walked with her out to my car, we got in, and I pointed us down the driveway. As we passed through the front gate, camera lights illuminated the interior of the car with a pop of white, but no more than twenty feet from the driveway we found the peaceful darkness of a Palos Verdes road. By the time we reached the bottom of the great hill, the car's heat was pumping nicely and I drove across the plain of Los Angeles in a drowsy half-sleep.

Rebecca requested that I drop her off at the Omni Hotel downtown, which wasn't far from my office. It catered to the corporations on Bunker Hill and charged exorbitant rates but apparently knew its clientele. I assumed that a complex filled with business types silently pounding out emails in their rooms or making brief phone calls with loved ones back home was the kind of quiet she needed.

I pulled into the loop of the Omni and waved off the valet who was eager to break the boredom of a late Sunday afternoon with a jaunt over to the parking garage.

Rebecca thanked me for the ride. I think I muttered something about an offer to help if she needed it but it probably didn't sound sincere. Her response confirmed that, but also that she was okay with it.

I found myself hovering as I watched her make her way inside. I saw her cross the expansive lobby and put the car into drive only when she disappeared into the bank of elevators.

It was a short drive back to my home in Eagle Rock, where I could finally put this day behind me. And yet I couldn't stop thinking about Rebecca and the fact that she never went to the hotel front desk. Only people who already have rooms go straight to the elevator bank.

ENGAGEMENT

I was back at the Omni Hotel the following morning.

Sitting on one of the sofas in the tiered lobby, I nervously scanned the room for any sign of Rebecca. I had already placed five calls to her, but she never answered. The messages I left weren't returned. I was approaching full-blown panic, not so much out of fear for Rebecca's safety as out of fear of losing my job.

It began earlier that morning with my regular touchbase with Pat Faber. The 6 a.m. start was deliberate as my boss liked to put people off their mark and see what kind of "mettle" they had when they weren't at their best. I often fantasized about becoming his boss and holding a 9 p.m. meeting to see how he operated two hours past his bedtime.

Surprisingly, Pat was already with someone when I got there. I heard a few insincere laughs from behind the door and knew the meeting was coming to a close.

Paul Darbin, one of the managers on my team, emerged. He swung his ponytail around to wish Pat goodbye and then saw me standing there. We exchanged a few awkward pleasantries before Pat made it clear that his time was more valuable than ours.

"Mr. Restic," he barked playfully and several decibels louder than needed for the empty office. "How was the weekend? Good?"

The second question saved me from having to answer the first. Pat wasn't interested in chatter about the rain, anyway. These meetings had a singular purpose—to make me feel uncomfortable—and therefore weekend banter was not on the agenda. He put his arm around me in an unfatherly way and led me into his office.

I had spent the better part of the prior evening and the drive in that morning figuring out how to get Pat to agree to hit the PAUSE button on the Power of One program and cancel that afternoon's presentation to the board. That fifteen-minute discussion would determine my future with the firm. And without the chance to rehearse with Julie, I felt woefully unprepared.

Getting Pat to agree to a postponement required a very delicate, very deliberate approach with carefully crafted language, which, after several minutes of buildup, would eventually reveal the reason for the delay: yesterday's tragic developments in Palos Verdes. This was not something that could be rushed.

"So what's with this murder at Julie St. Jean's house?" he asked before I could even sit down.

Pat shot me an "I still got it" smile.

"You beat me to it, Pat." I laughed, and matched the look of pride on his face. "Again!"

I filled him in on what little I knew but made sure he was aware that it was firsthand knowledge, i.e., that I had been working on a Sunday. I also purposely planted several set-up phrases like "lots of moving parts" and "searching for clarity" and "build the plane and fly it at the same time." These would soften the beachhead when I inevitably worked back to the conclusion that we would need to postpone the presentation to the board.

"Chuck, it all makes sense," he agreed.

"It's an unusual series of events, to say the least," I replied, pleased with how convincing I was.

"You've thought this through with great care, as usual," he continued.

I acknowledged the compliment but was wary of the fact that he gave one.

"As tempting as it is to hit the PAUSE button on this," he added, "let's press forward and discuss it with the management committee this afternoon. It's too critical."

I almost threw up for the second time in twenty-four hours.

"Pat," I choked, "that was going to be my recommendation."

For the next three hours I placed frantic calls to every phone number associated with Power of One. I left several messages on the room phone at the Omni Hotel. I sent urgent emails and rat-a-tat texts featuring a growing proportion of capital letters until the last one simply read: CALL ME!

All I got back was silence. I had no choice but to go over to the Omni and camp out in the lobby, where I hoped to run into Rebecca.

Sitting on one of the sofas in the upper level facing Grand Avenue, I replayed the events of that morning and regretted having underestimated Pat. I had lulled myself into thinking he was just a doddering old exec, but he still had his corporate manipulation wits about him. I needed to remember that if you can't see yourself being played, it's already too late. I was so absorbed in rethinking how I could have done better with Pat that I almost missed Rebecca.

She crossed the lower section of the lobby that led onto Olive Street. I called out her name, but she either didn't hear me over the din or she outright pretended not to hear me. The purposeful way she strode out the revolving doors and into the valet loop—almost too purposeful—made me think it was the latter.

I placed a call to her cell and watched as she grabbed her phone, checked the number, and pushed me straight to voicemail before jumping into an idling taxi.

I hustled down the stairs and ran out into the valet loop. I jumped into the back of the next taxi in line and instructed the driver to follow the car ahead of him.

"You serious?" he asked, making no move to heed my instructions.

I made up some lie about it being my wife and hinted that she might be doing something she shouldn't. I must have nicked some once-spurned scar because the driver said nothing as he put the car in gear and pulled in behind Rebecca's taxi.

Clearly, Power of One didn't think too highly of the contract with my firm, because after ignoring my call, Rebecca did a series of errands in and around downtown, none of which had anything to do with the presentation. She led us off the hill to a shopping center near the Staples Center, then to an office building that overlooked the downtown skyline from its perch on the north side of the freeway. It looked like a delivery because she entered with a shopping bag and emerged ten minutes later without it. She made a few more stops before concluding her journey at a medical mega-complex of Soviet-style structures in Lincoln Heights. This time she released her taxi and entered the maze of buildings.

No-showing on the presentation with the board was unacceptable. That kind of behavior was something you'd expect from Julie, the eccentric thinker of the group, not from the team's stalwart organizer. Power of One was always something of a nuisance to me but never a major concern. They were the equivalent of making my long glide into retirement a little more turbulent than necessary, but these latest developments threatened to take the plane down entirely.

I checked my watch and realized I needed to get back to the office for the presentation to the management committee. As I made the short return trip, I worked over in my head what I would say now that I had to give the speech without the benefit of Julie being there to defend her work.

Any hope of an easy time of it was dashed when

I entered the boardroom. Everyone was in attendance and looked eager to hear what I had to say, none more so than Pat, who sat there smiling like a gambler on the right side of a rigged fight.

Pat started the meeting by quickly briefing the committee before launching into the attack before I could even get through my prepared remarks.

"Do you still believe in Power of One?" he asked, in a masterful stroke of manipulation. The inclusion of *still* assumed I believed in them in the first place.

"I believe in what they're trying to accomplish," I replied.

"But are they going to get us over the goal line?" asked one of the committee members, unaware that we phased out football-related jargon several years earlier, following the national uproar against concussions.

"We're a unique firm, with unique needs," I replied, playing into their misplaced view that our firm was somehow special in the industry.

"Are we seeing the results in the engagement scores?" Pat challenged.

None of the committee members wanted to accept the dismal scores coming in from the recent employee survey. They couldn't figure out why no one shared the same level of satisfaction with the work they were doing (and more importantly, with the compensation that came with it). That disconnect led us to perpetually pursue solutions that didn't exist.

Sometimes it manifested itself in concrete ideas, like the continuous rollout of new Power of One programs. Or the extreme example of hiring a chief engagement officer, who after six months of staring at a blank screen, as she tried to figure out what she was actually supposed to do, just walked out and never returned. But mostly it meant people like me having to persuade everyone that our folks actually found passion in their meaningless work.

"Remember what Julie has always preached: 'Engagement is a journey, not an event.'"

I had thus far successfully avoided being pinned down, but it was only a matter of time before it happened. I could feel the frustration building. I flirted with losing the confidence of the committee members entirely.

Pat pounced.

"That brings up a good point," he said. "Where is Julie?"

"Yes, why isn't she here?" someone else piled on.

"Is this not important to her?" rang the chorus.

They served up the opening I needed to throw Julie and Power of One under the bus. But only a fool would have taken it. As much as I relished the opportunity to purge two decades' worth of complaints about them, I knew better than to pursue that tactic because ultimately, it would be used against me.

"Julie couldn't be here today," I began, "because she is working on something revolutionary."

Pat looked at me like I had lost my mind. But this time, he underestimated me.

I praised the new program for the lasting contributions it would make to the firm and to the individuals enrolled in it. I used all of the buzzwords of the truly disingenuous—*powerful, transformative, indelible,* and *significant.*

Pat looked disappointed. While he understood that ultimately I'd need to come back and prove these broad statements—something we both knew I couldn't do—he had tasted blood and wasn't ready to delay the finishing blow for another month until the next committee meeting.

"After all the failures they've had up to now," he started, "what gives you confidence that they will be successful this time around?"

All eyes settled on me. I paused a good ten seconds before responding.

"Let me tell you about someone," I began. "A guy early in his career driven only by the paycheck and the promise of promotion. His success was defined by personal advancement and although he accomplished that in spades, he wasn't a success in the truest sense of the word. But then he started working with Julie St. Jean. And he learned to harness the power of mindful collaboration. Only then did he realize what real success looked like—making others better."

I paused before delivering the obvious punch line.

"That someone was Chuck Restic."

Pat may have stared at me with an icy glare, but I got five heads nodding around him. He knew enough to not press it further.

"We look forward to reviewing their new *revolutionary* program," he said flatly.

Poor Pat would never get the chance to see it. I was going to get Power of One to resign long before that ever happened.

HORSE PILLS

A little-known secret of Corporate America is that nearly sixty percent of employees who are "let go" are never officially terminated. Most leave voluntarily to "pursue other opportunities outside the firm." That carefully crafted language indemnifies the company from future lawsuits and relieves it from paying unemployment claims. The reason so many associates agree to such lose-lose terms lies in the simple yet powerful technique of repeated humiliation.

The process begins benignly enough under the guise of helping the employee overcome an issue. But despite the countless regular meetings with HR and their manager, the issue never seems to get resolved. If it does, another issue crops up to replace it. These discussions begin to feel like they will never end. They won't.

An air of inevitability takes over, the process hurtling toward an outcome that always ends with their resignation. Of course, the associate is resigned long before the actual resignation comes in. Men have more pride and prove easier to shame than women, but both buckle eventually. Sociopaths are the only ones impervious to this technique, and with them you're better off just terminating and dealing with the lawsuit later.

I can't remember the number of times I navigated people through this process, but I do recall all of their faces on the day they finally "agreed" to part ways. The dignity of walking out of the building on their own was worth far more than the financial benefits of being terminated. The strangest part was that almost every one of them, often at the very end when they stood at the threshold to the elevator that would snuff out their career, thanked me for all I did for them.

Those ghosts still haunt me.

I had found my pressure point that afternoon when doing some research on Power of One. It was an interesting tidbit in a building management company's newsletter, announcing the exciting news that they would have a new tenant—an innovative consulting firm that would use the space to hold large lecture sessions complete with state-of-the-art interactive capabilities. The building was the very one Rebecca had visited earlier that morning. But something was off.

The date on the article was over a year earlier, which meant the lease was probably signed long before that. It looked like the Power of One women had overextended themselves, a common mistake of consultant outfits whose vision is grander than their ability to execute it.

Fiscal irresponsibility and financial peril were fertile ground for me to pressure them into resigning.

My plan was to lay out for Julie and Rebecca an augmentation of their program. Our firm was fully committed if—and this was where the stress point hit—they could deliver. I'd ask for certain things I knew their small outfit couldn't handle. I'd overwhelm them with requests for more and more deliverables until they reached a breaking point. Throughout, I'd constantly ask about their financial situation to apply more pressure.

I was certain it would work, but I didn't necessarily feel good about it. I just wanted this entire thing to be over.

I tried to beat the elevator rush by leaving a little early, but everyone else had the same idea. The busiest time was always ten minutes before people were supposed to leave for the day. As the throng was let out and flowed down into the parking garage and the standstill traffic that ultimately awaited, I peeled off and made the short walk over to the Omni Hotel.

After the third ring on the house phone, I was just about to give up when Rebecca answered. She sounded both exhausted and hopeful but settled on disappointed when it finally registered who was calling her.

"I'm downstairs," I said. "Can I come up?"

In her disorientation she accepted and gave me her room number.

Rebecca was slow to answer the door. She kept one hand on the doorframe, but it was more for her own support than any kind of gesture to keep me out. The poor lighting from the hallway mercilessly accentuated every hollow, every wrinkle in her face. She looked beaten down.

Five steps into the room, I found out why.

A quick glance told me she had been staying here for longer than one night. There were large suitcases and clothes everywhere. Boxes of Power of One training guides sat in a corner. And on the narrow secretary were a large water bottle, a glass, and a simple tray lined with orange prescription bottles. There were nearly fifteen of them in various sizes, neatly laid out with the lids all on but not closed tight. Labels faced out. The symmetry spoke of routine.

I pulled my eyes from the orange bottles and met Rebecca's gaze.

"I'm not sure that's any of your concern," she stated flatly.

My mind rushed back ten years to another tray of pills laid out in a remarkably similar fashion. This one sat on the counter in my father's kitchen in between the cupboard with the juice glasses and the sink. I remember him standing there every morning as he methodically made his way through the bottles. He'd stare out the little window over the sink at the climbing rosebush outside. The process took up to twenty minutes, particularly when he had to get up the fortitude to swallow the larger pills. Eventually, when he didn't have the strength to stand for such a long period, his routine moved from the kitchen counter to the couch. By the time he moved to the hospice bed in the living room, there was no longer any reason to take the pills.

"What do you want?" she asked.

What I wanted was to duck my head and leave. But now that I was there, I had to come up with a viable reason for dropping in unannounced. I began vaguely with some comments about "progress toward mutual goals" and "getting traction on core deliverables" and got vaguer still the more I spoke. The clearest solution to the hole I was digging was to just put down the shovel. Instead, I doubled down and rambled on for another three minutes.

"Huh?" she replied.

Rebecca's one-word response perfectly captured her bewilderment and the fact that I had used many words to say absolutely nothing.

"Why don't you tell me why you're really here," she challenged.

"Like I said, I just wanted to—"

"*Really* here," she interrupted.

"I thought we could regroup on the program," I started again, but Rebecca wasn't buying any of it.

"Are you trying to fire us?"

"Fire?" I repeated incredulously.

Rebecca was smart enough to realize that the repetition of her question squarely confirmed that that was the exact reason for my visit. I watched her pallid complexion get a little less so. She regained some of her balance, her eyes got some vigor back in them, and in that brief instant she looked healthy again.

The demonstration proved life's great motivator after fear was anger.

"We're not quitting," she stated.

"I understand you guys are going through a lot right now—"

"Do you, now?"

"Well maybe not everything—"

"Get out," she hissed.

We had officially passed the point at which all hopes of rescuing the discussion were lost. It was best to heed her request and live to fight another day.

"I'm sorry," I muttered pathetically.

I made my way toward the door. As I opened it, I was greeted by a deep voice, one far deeper than Julie St. Jean's. Attached to it was a short-nosed gun pointed right at my stomach.

OKAY

"Where's Fitch?" asked the man.

He couldn't have been more than five-and-a-half-feet tall, with a neck so thick that no standard collar could wrap around it. His physique was in the bowling ball category—round and hard. He was probably in his sixties and looked like he had a lot of vinegar left in him.

"Who?" I asked.

"Fitch," the man repeated. "I'm looking for Jimmy Fitch."

"I, I think you have the wrong room…" I said, turning for confirmation from Rebecca.

"Who is it?" she asked behind me. "What does he want?"

I was obstructing her view of the man and, more importantly, of the gun pointed at my stomach. Therefore, she didn't feel the need to tread lightly around him. If anything, she was overly antagonistic.

"Tell him to buzz off."

"I think you have the wrong room," I said softly. "Probably just an honest mistake."

"Both of you get out," Rebecca sniped.

The man took that as his invitation to come inside. I found myself backing into the room and trying to get as far from the barrel of the gun as possible.

"What'd I just say?" Rebecca shouted. "I told you to get out."

"Everyone just relax," I said, in an attempt to defuse the situation. No one likes to be told to relax, and this man was no exception. He flicked his free hand and shoved me backward. My foot caught the edge of the bed and I tumbled dramatically to the floor.

"Jesus! Take it easy," I cried, in a voice a little too whiny for my own liking.

The man stood over me as he surveyed the room. His eyes darted from one object to the next, looking for something familiar, but with each turn of his head he grew less certain. He blinked his way to the conclusion that he did indeed have the wrong room. He didn't apologize. He turned and quietly exited.

I cautiously followed him to the door and locked it. The fish-eye view out the peephole showed the hallway was empty, but I couldn't be sure. I hoped Rebecca had forgotten about kicking me out earlier, even just for a minute to give me time to put more distance between me and the armed man.

"Do you know that guy?" I asked.

She shook her head.

"What about the man he was looking for? I think he said the name Fitch?"

Again, she shook her head.

I glanced around. Suddenly this little box of a corporate hotel room situated on a heavily patrolled hill in downtown no longer felt very safe. Even the heavy door with three forms of locks and latches looked ominous.

"Maybe he had the wrong room," I said, but my tone felt like it needed convincing. It could have been a coincidence and not actually connected to the murder of the caricaturist, but those sorts of coincidences don't happen too often.

I pulled out my phone.

"What are you doing?" she asked.

"I'm calling the police," I told her.

As I raised it to my ear, her hand rested gently on my wrist. Rebecca met my gaze and quietly shook her head. I ended the call before it was picked up.

I let silence fill a few minutes.

"What's going on?" I finally asked.

"I don't know," she said.

"Where's Julie?"

"I don't know," came the same reply.

"Are you worried?" I asked.

Rebecca shot me a look that made me regret stating the obvious. She was worried but not necessarily out of fear for Julie's safety.

"The police spoke to our gardener today," Rebecca explained. "He says he saw Julie leaving the house on Saturday afternoon."

"She's a suspect," I finished for her.

"*Person of interest*," she corrected. "They would like to talk to her." After a moment she added, "As would I."

My urge to help was countered by the realization that there wasn't anything I could actually do other than offer bits of advice that she already knew.

"You should at least tell the PV police about this," I instructed. "And consider another place to stay."

"I'll move to another room," Rebecca responded, ignoring my first suggestion.

"If he found this room he could find another."

"You're right," she said, but not in a way that meant she would do anything about it.

"You should really call the police," I continued. But she wasn't listening anymore. She just sat on the edge of the bed and stared at a spot on the carpet that held no answers.

"I'm sorry, Rebecca."

I made a move to leave.

"Okay," I heard her say behind me.

When I turned, I saw an image I knew too well and had seen too often. It was the one I'd seen sitting across from me when some poor bastard decided their best option was to leave the firm voluntarily, the same look they had when making the "dead man walking" march to the elevator bank. It was the look of complete resignation.

"Okay," she repeated, "we'll quit the contract."

I left with what I came for but there was no joy in the victory.

ANOTHER WALK TO THE ELEVATOR

The following morning, I had my monthly touch-base with Paul Darbin and the outside private investigator we used on everything from background checks on job candidates to surveillance work on false disability claims. Badger (this was a self-appointed nickname that I reluctantly had to use with him) was undergoing a bit of a transformation ever since I started holding these meetings at the office and since we started giving him more important work. As if sensing that he needed to professional-up his image, he traded in the acid-wash jeans for a suit that unfortunately looked like the one his father was buried in. He also attempted to upgrade his vocabulary in these office sessions, but invariably succeeded only in further butchering his already well-slaughtered use of the English language.

"Hold up, chief," he said over Paul's attempt to move on to the next agenda item. "I'd like to reconnoiter that last topic."

Paul once complained to me about Badger's use of the term *chief*, feeling it was grossly insensitive to the ancestors of our great land. I encouraged Paul to take the issue up with Badger personally, not because I thought he was right but because I knew what would happen. I had made that mistake before and was subjected to a long dissertation on how Badger's mother was one-eighth Cherokee and suffered many an injustice growing up among the *yonega*, a derogatory term for white people. I later found out he was a tract-housing kid from Lakewood, but why ruin a good story? What mattered was that he believed that story, as evidenced by his tear-streaked cheeks when he told it to me.

"My own Trail of Tears," he said, wiping his face.

I smiled at how much he grated on Paul. Pushing my colleague's buttons was fast becoming one of my favorite pastimes. We had always been "friendly" rivals at the firm, but ever since I took over the role as head of the group and Paul started reporting to me, I found myself going out of my way to make his life miserable. I justified these actions by recalling how unprofessional he was when we both applied for my current position. He did everything in his power to undercut me, often with false information. I wanted to believe I was above petty retribution, but in Paul's case I made an exception.

Paul had once tried to replace Badger with a private investigator of a more "appropriate caliber," code for someone more polished. Badger's edges were rough, but at his core he was honest and a hell of a good inves-

tigator. I eventually denied Paul's request and to show
no hard feelings, I put him in charge of managing the
Badger account.

"One more stealth item," Paul said, using the term
for a topic not on the approved agenda. "Have you been
following the story about the murder in Palos Verdes of
the woman who worked for Power of One?"

"Vaguely familiar," I said, and purposely checked
my watch, which signaled that this topic would not be
worth the time it was about to take. Paul either missed
my cue or purposely ignored it.

"Our very own Julie St. Jean is wanted for questioning," he continued. "But it doesn't look like they know
her whereabouts."

Paul had every right to probe this topic but for some
reason I found myself deflecting. I let my silence show
how much of a non-issue this was for me and even
went so far as to start piling up the handouts from the
meeting and putting the cap on my pen. It all said one
thing—this meeting was over.

"This person of interest works for you guys?" Badger
piped up.

I tried to shut Badger up with a cold glare. He caught
it and seemed to understand.

"This is clearly upsetting you, Chuck," he said. "Tells
me I need to get to the bottom of it."

"I agree," Paul quickly piled on.

"Guys, let's be prudent here. I understand your concern, but we already have a full list of action items, so
we don't need to be creating new work for ourselves.

I'll add it to the parking lot," I said, using another term whose literal meaning was to "park" a topic for later discussion but whose effective meaning was to put it somewhere and never talk about it again.

"We should consider looking into it," Paul continued. "Pat's always telling us to challenge the conventional thinking."

I studied Paul.

I had wondered how Pat had gotten word of the murder at Julie's house so quickly, and now I had my answer: Paul had told him. This was one aspect of Paul's repertoire that I couldn't underestimate. Passive-aggressive undermining came naturally to him.

I could have told Paul that Power of One would no longer be engaged by our firm but I held back. It seemed safer to play along until the breakup was official and well-communicated to the higher-ups.

I told Badger to put it on his list.

"This is my number-one priority," he pronounced. He somehow forgot that he had made this claim twice already in the meeting. Badger's list of priorities read horizontally because every task was slotted in at the top position.

"Thank you," I said, and watched Paul smirk, so proud of his maneuvering skills. I let him enjoy it, then added, "Add ColorNalysis to that list, too."

Paul jerked his head so fast his ponytail whipped around and nearly hit him in the face.

"Why, why do we need to do that?" he stammered.

"Contingency planning," I said. "If your concerns

over Power of One are confirmed, we'll need a backup plan. ColorNalysis is the likely successor to guide associate development programs, wouldn't you agree?"

Of course he would agree, because he'd been pushing us to replace Julie's firm with this one for nearly five years. Paul was one of their disciples, going so far as to travel with his *lifemate*—a term he coined to justify a long-term relationship with a woman who wouldn't agree to his prenuptial agreement—to a three-day ColorNalysis retreat in Sedona so they could better understand each other. He made our firm pay for his half of the bill.

ColorNalysis was another outfit selling the same nonsense but presented under the banner of neuroscience to lend it some validity. They used brain mapping to chart your personality type on a patented grid that looked like a four-color Rorschach test. This color card became the guide from which your individualized development plan was generated, with the goal of helping you focus on the areas that needed stretching. I marveled at this machine's uncanny ability to always pinpoint one area—color—in major need of extensive (read: expensive) one-on-one counseling.

"They're on my list," Badger announced. But before he could tell us yet again that it was his number-one priority, I stole his thunder.

"Badger, let's put that one at the top," I instructed.

I felt bad for denying Badger the pleasure of his usual pronouncement, but it was worth it to see the pallor of Paul's face. ColorNalysis, like all these outfits, had to have some skeletons in their closet. These were rarely deal breakers, but Paul's reaction gave me pause. Maybe we should be looking into them after all.

The meeting was over, but I asked Badger to hold on for a minute. Paul nervously looked back as he left my office. It was a cheap move on my part—no one wants to feel left out of a private discussion—but this time I had a legitimate request for Badger. But before I could get to it, he surprised me.

"I assume you don't want me to do any actual work on these consultants?" he asked.

I smiled and gave him an approving slap on the back, and got a whiff of his cheap aftershave, which failed to mask the odor of whatever damp towel he used to store his suit in.

"Badger's no dummy," he said, shifting to the third person, which signaled an elevated level of pride in his own abilities.

"No, he's not." I played along. "But I actually do want you to look into Julie St. Jean. Personal reasons," I added to address his confused look.

"Ahhhh," he mused, and gave me a wink.

"Not that personal," I corrected. "Just dig up what you can."

Rebecca came by the office that afternoon to sign the documents that would officially end our two firms' relationship. I had left a clause open that would offer some remuneration for early termination, but to my surprise, she turned it down.

"If we're not doing any work," she said, "we shouldn't be paid."

It was probably better that she declined it because the penny-pinchers would have many questions for me once they discovered the extra payment.

"Where should I sign?" she asked.

It all felt too rushed, and I felt a pang of guilt that it had to be under these circumstances. I found myself finding ways to delay the inevitable.

"Any updates on Julie?" I asked.

There was some news but none of it was good. Rebecca relayed in a very matter-of-fact manner the call she had gotten from the Palos Verdes police informing her that they had found Julie's Bentley at a Union Station long-term parking lot. They believed it had been there since Saturday. So far, closed-circuit cameras hadn't turned up any more information. It meant one of two things—Julie was either in trouble or on the run.

"How are you holding up?"

"I could answer, but it would just be a throwaway response."

I nodded.

"Sorry. I don't mean to be so dismissive."

"It's okay. It was a meaningless question."

"The one thing, Chuck?" she said. "The thing I can't get my arms around? How fast it all unraveled."

Rebecca had likely used my first name countless times in the past but there was something about this instance that struck me deeply. Perhaps it was having it

linked to such a brutally honest reflection from someone I hardly knew.

"I think I can help you," I blurted out.

Later, I realized this was my intention all along. It
was hard to put into words but I just felt a need to try to
help her. It led me to deflect Paul's probing of Power of
One, it led me to request Badger's assistance, and it led
me to make the offer to help when I should have been
getting her to sign the termination documents.

The way I said it, however, and the way Rebecca
looked at me, it felt like both of us needed convincing.

"Help me with what?"

"Find Julie."

At least she didn't laugh. But she didn't accept the
offer, either. Instead, she thought about it for a minute,
then asked an odd question.

"What do you think of me and Julie?"

Before I could answer with some fluffy response
that masked the true feelings beneath the words, she
appended her question.

"What do you *really* think of me and Julie?"

"I think you could guess," I said, laughing.

"I want to hear you say it."

"Well, for starters," I began casually.

Rebecca looked at me like she was ready for the
truth.

"I think you and Julie are certifiable cranks. I'd even
go so far as to say you're a couple of con artists. You
haven't done anything to warrant even a penny of the
money that's been paid to you. All of your programs are

just packaged-up gibberish. And, really, the only thing that's kept me from losing my mind all these years while sitting in your endless sessions is the dream of one day getting to fire your sorry asses."

The words were even more satisfying to express than the countless times I had imagined saying them. Even Rebecca seemed to find some level of enjoyment out of them as she studied me with a wry smile. But she had another view to share.

"'A lonely, frustrated man,'" she said. "That's what Julie calls you. I'd probably add a few more adjectives."

"I bet you would."

"You know I'm sick," she said. "Big 'S' sick."

It was a subtle jab at the corporate world for its habit of signaling something of importance by actually saying that the word was capitalized.

"You'll be fine," I said.

"That's not what I meant."

There was defiance behind her words and a clear signal that she loathed anything approaching pity.

"Altruism is overrated," I told her. "And I believe I can actually help you."

"What about this?" she said, pointing to the paperwork before her.

"We'll figure it out later."

I put the unsigned documents back in the folder.

Later, as we walked out to the elevator, I thought I heard her whisper: "There's really no one else."

That could have meant no one else in her life, no one else who could help her, or both.

RENO OR BUST

I cashed in an RO (Remote Office) card, which allowed employees to work a few days a month out of their homes. Everyone loved these days because without the distractions of the office setting, they were able to be much more "productive." In practice, that meant chiming in on a few emails to prove you were working, but otherwise, you were free to do whatever you wanted—play golf, do some Christmas shopping, or just watch *I Love Lucy* reruns.

I used my RO day to begin the search for Julie St. Jean.

Rebecca had a morning treatment, so I picked her up at the chemo center in Lincoln Heights and we headed over to the Omni Hotel so I could help her pack. The one condition I had stipulated before starting to help her was that she agree to switch hotels. As Rebecca slid the keycard into the slot and opened the door, I think both of us expected someone on the other side. I feared another run-in with the bowling ball man; I'm sure she secretly hoped to find Julie lounging on the bed.

The room was empty.

Rebecca packed her things while I made several trips to the car. The exile from the Palos Verdes home—self-imposed or otherwise—had clearly been a long one. The rift I imagined she had had with Julie widened with each additional bag I loaded into the trunk of my car.

"You can take those boxes down," she instructed while she dumped the tray of prescription bottles into her purse. Nothing is more unmistakable than the rattle of pills in plastic bottles.

I recognized the boxes stacked in the corner as containing the binders for the latest Power of One workshop. It was an unnerving reminder that I still needed to resolve the issue at work with them. As I did with most problems in need of immediate attention, I decided to let it marinate and hoped a magic solution would appear later.

"Jesus," I yelped, as I hefted the first box of binders onto the bellhop cart. Who knew nonsense weighed so much, I mused, massaging my lower back. That's when I noticed the red light on the room phone.

"There's a message," I told Rebecca.

She looked at me.

"All of mine were from the other day. You never returned them."

Rebecca ignored my jab and hurried over to the phone. I watched her expression go from hopeful to disappointed as she listened to the voicemail.

"Just the front desk," she said. "They have my umbrella." She gave a puzzled look at the door, where an umbrella was leaning in the corner. "Must be a mistake," she reasoned.

On the final load out, I swung by the front desk but no one there seemed to recall a missing umbrella. The lost and found box didn't contain one either.

"Try the valet," the receptionist suggested. "Folks sometimes leave things in the courtesy cars. They have their own lost and found."

That piqued my interest. I recalled the development that Julie's Bentley was found parked at Union Station. The police likely assumed she fled the city on a train. But Union Station was only a short walk from the Omni Hotel. Julie might have used that as a ruse to throw the police off her trail.

I made my way out to the main entrance and asked around until I found a valet who worked on Saturday.

"A guest used one of the courtesy cars," I told him. "Do they get them through you guys?"

"We pull them up from the garage."

"If I gave you a description of a guest would you be able to get the car she used?" I asked.

"If it's still here," he said.

I described Julie St. Jean to him but didn't get past the words "woman with white hair."

"Talks like a man?" he asked. "Yeah, I remember her. Nice lady," which meant she had tipped him well. "She took the Lincoln."

"Was she with anyone?"

"Not that I remember."

"How long did she have the car?"

"I never saw her come back but the office in the garage would know."

"Or you could get that information for me," I suggested, and made a move for my wallet. The punk waited for me to actually get it out and start thumbing through the larger bills before he replied.

"Happy to be of service," he said, smiling.

"Do you use this bank?" I asked Rebecca.

We delayed checking her in to another hotel until we followed up on the leads from the navigation system in the hotel courtesy car. I was able to narrow down the timeframe when Julie had used the vehicle so that Rebecca and I could retrace her steps on Saturday afternoon in the hopes that a narrative would emerge. One did, but it wasn't exactly a welcome one.

The trail began at a chain drugstore in Highland Park and then led to the mall in Glendale. After that it was a sporting goods store just north on Pacific. The following entry brought us across the 134 to an address on Lake Avenue in Pasadena. It housed an old bank with a name that recalled the agrarian times of its founding. The only thing "agricultural" remaining in Pasadena these days were the pots of organic basil growing on condominium balconies.

Rebecca shook her head as we idled in the red zone

across the street from the bank.

"I've never used it."

A clear but disheartening picture of the hours after Lois was murdered was forming—it was of someone preparing to go on the run. The next stop put to rest any doubts I might have had of that fact.

The address led us to a large shopping center in El Monte, just off the 10 Freeway. It was anchored by a car dealership and ringed by auto accessory parts stores and cut-rate insurance outfits. We stared at the rows of new and "like new" cars on display and the markdown prices screaming in fluorescent green numbers across their windshields.

"Maybe they'll tell us what kind of car she bought," Rebecca suggested, pointing at the small collection of cheap suits huddling under large golf umbrellas. The pack had already picked up our scent and was starting to disperse.

Rebecca had apparently come to the same conclusion as I had about Julie going on the lam.

"They might not give us information on a customer," I said, watching the chubby alpha male make a beeline for our car.

"We could bribe them," said Rebecca.

"Have to figure out which is the crooked one."

I watched the approaching man lean over to give a peekaboo smile. He looked at us like wounded prey that he couldn't wait to get to overpay on a vehicle with a dirty title. Naturally, that car would be pitched as having had a single, elderly owner who kept it in a covered garage and only took it out for weekly bingo nights.

"Easier to pick out the honest one," Rebecca reasoned, and got out to greet the man. She cut right to the chase. I watched her describe Julie with an outstretched hand denoting her height and a sweep of the hair describing her white mane. The man nodded and disappeared inside. He returned fifteen minutes later with a slip of paper, which was exchanged for some agreed-upon amount of money.

"A 2001 tan Saturn," Rebecca told me.

This was the side of Rebecca I knew best. It was the only side I knew, really. While Julie St. Jean was the face of, and brains behind, Power of One, Rebecca made sure it all ran well. For that she was given the thankless label of "the person who gets stuff done."

In a lot of ways this arrangement was no different than the one I endured at work. The common complaint among the "idea guys" in upper management was that they needed more time to strategize, but they were constantly being dragged into too much execution. The worst label anyone could levy on another leader was to refer to them as "tactical."

I deeply resented this view. As someone who'd made a career with the proverbial shovel digging the proverbial ditch—albeit our ditch was in a climate-controlled skyscraper and didn't involve any real physical labor—I vowed that should I ever get to their level, I would do things differently. Recently granted a new role in upper management, I proceeded to do no such thing.

Strategizing was just too damn easy.

But I still felt guilty. And because of that I found my-self overextending my role when I offered to knock on the door of the final address on the list from the navigation system. The house was on a flat, unkempt street in Bald-win Park. The rains had brought lush patches of weeds to its otherwise barren front yard and washed away a year's worth of dust from the once-white stucco walls.

I was starting to regret my offer to take the lead. This wasn't the best of neighborhoods and the house itself was less than inviting. Near the door was a large sign that informed trespassers they weren't wanted. And if that warning wasn't heeded, there was another sign fea-turing a German shepherd who didn't look the friendly type. A third sign lay against the railing and appeared to advertise a for-sale-by-owner vehicle.

I skirted several puddles on my way to the entrance. Faced with a larger puddle, I secretly wished I hadn't worn my nice shoes. I attempted a casual hop but came up a half-foot short and a splash of muddy water soaked my pant bottoms.

"Damn it," I muttered, wiping at some of the large spots with my hand. When I finally looked up I was greeted with a blank stare from a rail-thin Latino with a shaved head. He stood under the overhang of the roof and the rain had drawn a dark line a few inches from where his bare feet stood on a dry step. He carried a baby in his arms. He or she lay limply against the man, lost in a deep sleep. The few drops of rain that caught the pudgy bare leg didn't seem to bother either of them. For some reason, the man was more threatening holding a newborn than he would have been holding a weapon.

"I'm looking for someone. Older lady with white hair, talks like a man. About this high," I said, and gestured up to a midpoint on my chest. "I think she might have visited you on Saturday." And just for the hell of it, I added, "She's wanted in connection with a murder."

Of all the responses he could have made, this one surprised me.

"That *abuelita* couldn't kill no one," he said dismissively.

"So you know her?" I asked.

"I wouldn't say I know her, but I talked to her," he explained.

The man suddenly got very chatty. He told me how he'd run a classified ad for a portable grill that Julie was apparently interested in. He described the exchange, but there weren't any details of much significance, except that he did drop repeated bits about the long drive to Reno she was apparently planning.

"She mentioned needing chains on her car tires or something," he said. "I'm from LA, man. I don't know shit about the snow."

I began to feel bad for the baby, whose legs were turning a splotchy crimson in the cold air. I interrupted the man and thanked him for his time.

Back in the car, I turned the heat up. My clothes were now wet from standing in the drizzle. I cupped both hands over one of the vents.

"Well?" Rebecca asked.

"Well, we know what kind of car she's really driving,"

I said, pointing to the for-sale sign. "A 2003 silver Nissan Sentra. And we know the one place she isn't heading for is Reno, Nevada."

Julie would have known that buying a car from a dealer, even a disreputable one like the lot we visited earlier, would have required certain documents that she couldn't afford to produce if she wanted to keep her movements secret. A private purchase made much more sense. I reasoned that she met the man at a public place and the dealer parking lot right off the freeway made a likely spot.

"Then what's this the guy gave me?" Rebecca asked, holding up the slip of paper from the used-car salesman.

"He made a quick hundred off of you," I told her.

"It was only fifty," she said, but still looked disappointed.

The transaction between Julie and the vehicle's owner probably happened right there in the lot. And given the nature of the transaction, it should have ended there. But according to the time on the courtesy car's navigation, she went to the seller's home address two hours later. I had an idea what that could mean but didn't share it with Rebecca.

My suspicion was that there were two transactions that day—one for the car and one for something else that required a little time to get. That chatty seller with the obvious attempts to throw me off Julie's scent convinced me that whatever she bought wasn't legal and didn't require an ID and a three-day background check to purchase.

CADILLACS

We drove north on the 605 toward the foothills which were shrouded in rain clouds. The road technically ran right through the San Gabriel River, but after decades of engineering marvels, the river had been transformed into a series of dams, watersheds, and reservoirs that channeled the rain off the mountains and ran it all the way to the ocean. Normally bone dry, the sun-bleached boulders were buried beneath gray water, and the sluices that I once thought were permanently rusted shut were now open to relieve the pressure building behind them.

Our last stop that day didn't come from the list of addresses on the navigation system. Earlier that morning, I'd logged into my firm's digital document center and pulled up any and everything we had on Julie St. Jean. For once, my firm's hyperparanoia of being sued actually came in handy.

Manic documentation of everything we ever did was a hallmark of the company. We once had an entire floor dedicated to file storage, but when the cost became unmanageable, we went through the arduous task of digitizing every sheet of paper once stored there. Now I had every document at my fingertips with a quick search in the database.

I started with thirty years of invoices paid out to Power of One. This caused me to waste twenty minutes calculating and then resenting the annualized gross income made off the back of my firm. I stopped counting when it reached the eight-figure mark. That was an impressive amount to fritter away, if my assumptions about their financial state were accurate.

I then moved to the personnel files and found the original W-9 that Julie had first filled out when she was a one-woman shop doing executive coaching with Pat Faber. The tax form had some very valuable information, including her social security number, her city of birth (Vero Beach, Florida), and the date she was born. I had to check the math when figuring out her age because it didn't seem right. By this record she was nearly seventy years old, but to me she didn't look a day over fifty. I found myself subconsciously touching the sides of my head where I knew the gray hairs were coming in faster than I wanted them to. As a septuagenarian, Julie had thirty years on me and far more grays but she also looked like she could take me handily in a fight. The last bit of helpful information on the W-9 was an address in Sierra Madre, a hippie enclave nestled in the mountains just northeast of Pasadena.

We took the road up, a straight two-mile stretch of such perfect pitch that if you rolled a marble from the top it might not stop until it hit San Diego. I watched the outside temperature gauge on the dashboard as it dropped one degree for every half-mile we traveled. Oaks lining the road slowly gave way to towering pines and foreshadowed the mountain retreat that awaited us. At the crest was the L-shaped downtown, forever a decade late in whatever trendy fad was happening down below.

"Says to keep heading north," Rebecca instructed.

Instead, I turned west.

"You're supposed to take that street all the way up."

"Shortcut," I said, even though I had never been in this town before and didn't know any of the streets. I wanted to get off the main drag and onto quieter streets to see if the Cadillac was still behind us.

I'd noticed it back in Baldwin Park and then again as we got off the freeway. There weren't that many old Coupe DeVilles driving around Los Angeles outside of the occasional cholo lowrider, so it was easy to spot. I couldn't quite get a good look at the driver but it appeared to be the same bowling ball of a man who barged into Rebecca's hotel room. As I made a series of turns that got us deep into a residential area, I glanced in the mirror to see if it was still back there.

"Is someone following us?" Rebecca asked.

"I don't think so," I lied.

I directed us back toward our initial destination but

made periodic checks in the mirror to see if the Caddie had reappeared. It hadn't.

The roads narrowed as we entered the part of Sierra Madre that clawed its way into the foothill canyons. A log sign indicated the fire warning level and for once it was firmly pointing to green. The prior year, a careless hiker had caused a small fire that took out a stretch of the forest and a few houses. That was modest in terms of damage, but the bigger danger came after the flames were put out. The scorched earth, already bone dry from years of drought, had nothing to hold it in place without the trees and their roots. All it would take was one extended rainstorm to loosen the earth from the bedrock and half the mountain would come down like a lava flow of black mud. And the houses would come with it.

Unlike the perfect symmetry of the grid down below, up here they put the streets where nature dictated. The result was a narrowing lane constantly bending around giant boulders, and only when that wasn't feasible did you see the drill holes where the dynamite had been inserted. We got to the street indicated on Julie's original W-9 form and were greeted with a temporary sign that said only residents' cars were allowed beyond that point. It didn't look like two cars could fit on the road anyway, so I pulled over under a set of sprawling sycamores and parked. The rain collected on their large brown leaves sent big drops down onto the roof of my car, each one sounding like a muzzled gunshot.

We were going to have to make it the rest of the way on foot, but one glance in Rebecca's direction caused me to reconsider. She didn't look well, despite her protests that she was fine. There was an ancient general-store-style coffee shop at the beginning of the street, and I suggested we grab a bite to eat. She was more tired than I thought because she acquiesced without much of a fight.

The place didn't look like it had been redecorated in fifty years. There were about ten tables topped with picnic-checkered vinyl tablecloths. An entire wall was covered in perforated board and shelving that displayed cheap ceramics and other used knickknacks for sale. A potbellied stove in the corner provided the heat for the entire place.

Several locals' gazes lingered on us but they quickly returned to their coffees and conversation. Rebecca and I sat at the counter on a couple of stools. The elbows of countless customers had worn perfectly spaced out circles across the length of the Formica top. A mirrored rack opposite us held coffee mugs with names inscribed on them, which I assumed were for regulars. I spotted one with "Julie" on it, but doubted it belonged to the woman we sought.

An old man behind the counter approached with a pot of coffee and laid out two mugs without names on them. It was assumed that anyone sitting at the counter was there for one purpose—a cup of joe. We didn't disagree.

"You want menus?" he asked, but before I could answer he informed us that they didn't have any. Instead, he pointed to a chalkboard on the wall with about six items to choose from. We each ordered soup and a sandwich.

"Been open a long time?" I asked when the old man returned with our food. He didn't dignify my question with a response. Instead, he held up the pot of coffee as an offer for a refill. I nodded, then asked him if he knew someone from this area.

"Know lots of people," he informed me.

"Her name is Julie St. Jean?"

I detected a slight hiccup in his otherwise smooth coffee pour.

"Sounds familiar," he replied, but I got the sense he knew more than he was letting on.

"She lives up the road here, right?"

"Used to," he corrected.

"When did she move out?" I asked.

"I just work here," he said, laughing, and filled up Rebecca's mug. "I'm not the Hall of Records."

He tried to play it off as a joke, but my questions were clearly unwanted. He found something more pressing to do and left us to our lunch.

Atmosphere can sometimes trump quality, as it did when the warm shop with the woodstove pumping heat on our backs somehow managed to make two shitty grilled cheese sandwiches and bowls of canned tomato soup taste like the ones from fond childhood memories.

"Like my mom used to make," I said, holding up the half-eaten sandwich. "Where'd you grow up, Rebecca?"

"A long ways from here."

I wasn't surprised by the vague response. We'd spent

the better part of the day together but our conversations never managed to go very deep. Even the foolproof method of two individuals sitting in traffic in a locked car couldn't get her to open up. It was deliberate, but I didn't know why.

"Where's Julie from?" I pressed, even though I already knew she was born in Vero Beach.

"Back east," she said casually.

"Everything but Hawaii qualifies for that," I replied.

"I can't remember. Florida, I think."

"You guys *are* married, right?" I laughed.

I was being a smartass but there was a legitimate question in there, one I had been asking other same-sex couples for years. Once the state recognized gay marriage—and the health insurance benefits that came with it—there was an influx of requests by our employees to put their significant others onto the company health plan. It fell upon my group to weed out the frauds, an impossible task of determining if couples were "legitimate" in the traditional sense of the term or if an employee was just seizing the opportunity to offer his loser roommate free health insurance. The answers Rebecca gave me were not indicative of two people in a lifelong bond of love and devotion.

"How long have you been in the Palos Verdes house?"

"Seven years come March. Well, Julie lived in the house long before I moved in," she clarified.

"But you two have known each other for a long time."

"Since the eighties."

"And together for…?"

"Since the eighties."

I wanted to define my question by adding the word "romantically" but decided against it.

"Julie never mentioned Sierra Madre?"

"Not that I can remember," she answered.

By my records, Julie had lived at the address up the road—or claimed she lived here on the W-9—for almost seven years. It seemed unrealistic that someone wouldn't mention it at least once, even in a casual conversation. And it was equally odd that her wife lacked any curiosity about the discovery at all.

"You know, you're allowed more than three words per answer."

I said it lightly but couldn't mask my growing frustration.

"I don't like talking about myself," she said.

"I'm just trying to learn more about Julie. The more I do, the better the chances that we find her."

"You're curious about her but I don't think knowing her past is going to help you understand her." She spun on the stool to face me. "I'm not trying to be difficult. You can ask all you want about me and Julie but just know that we never delved into the past, so I won't be much help. Our relationship is very much of the present."

"That sounds like consultant gobbledygook," I said. It also sounded like more Julie nonsense, but I let that go unsaid. "You're telling me you and Julie never asked each other about your lives before you met each other?"

Rebecca shook her head. "The past lies, too, you know."

I called for the check. The old man had his back to us but responded very quickly, as if anticipating the request. I wasn't too surprised because the entire time we were there, I got the sense that he was listening in on our conversation.

BUTTERFLIES

We made our way up the street on foot. I now understood the reason for the restrictions—the road was only wide enough for one car and there was nowhere to turn around. Even the "driveways" were short strips where one could barely pull a car in with enough room to spare to not have your bumper ripped off by passing vehicles.

The homes were packed tightly together and featured small porches and chalet-like carved trim, vestiges of their former lives as weekend hunting lodges. Wealthy families from Pasadena and Los Angeles would come up here to escape the heat of summer and potentially bag a deer or maybe just catch some trout for dinner.

We passed several homeowners installing long planks at the end of their driveways. I realized that all of the homes had this peculiar addition—a set of pipes at each side of the driveway entrance into which the heavy planks could slide to form a temporary wall. I asked one of the homeowners about it. He gestured warily toward the top of the hill.

"Keeps the mud out," he said.

The street suddenly felt more menacing, as if around any of the bends could come a flash flood of mud that would sweep us down the hill. The newly formed walls made the whole thing into a sort of channel and blocked off all attempts of escape. I wanted off that road.

The house was a green and brown structure, a little more worse for wear than its neighbors. The driveway was empty and there were no lights on inside. We walked up the short set of stairs to the front porch, whose boards sagged slightly under our feet. There was no doorbell. I pulled open a dusty screen door and knocked on the door behind it.

"Looks abandoned," Rebecca said behind me.

I wasn't ready to give up yet. I followed the porch around the length of the house and descended ten steps to a concrete landing in a micro-backyard that was small even by Brooklyn-brownstone standards. A moss-covered oak tree ensured this area never got sun. The run-off channel bordered the back of the house and drowned out all sounds.

The half-basement underneath the house had at some point been converted into a living space. I cupped my hands over the glass door and peered inside. The room couldn't have been more than twelve by fifteen feet. It was an odd shape as it followed the contours of the bedrock it was built into. The far "wall" was actually a giant boulder, cleaned and sealed and unmoving until the next Ice Age pushed it farther down the hill.

The room wasn't furnished but it was decorated in a sort of Turkish theme with woven rugs, long cushions on the floor, and a large number of throw pillows. All it needed was a brass hookah and yataghan to complete the Ottoman aesthetic.

As eccentric as all this was, it was the artwork that caught my eye.

I tried the door handle and found it unlocked. I entered the room and studied the drawings on the wall. They were mostly abstract, of what appeared to be butterflies, rendered in familiar charcoal by a familiar hand. Although not signed, they were undoubtedly drawn by the visioning artist, Lois.

There had to be almost twenty versions of the same butterfly drawing, each with a date inscribed in the corner. Some were taped to the wall, but given the limited space, many more were piled on the floor. I picked up a stack and flipped through them. Only when I came upon a graphic portrait of a woman lying on her back, her legs slightly open, her eyes as naked as the rest of her body, did I realize that the other drawings didn't depict butterflies but something much more salacious.

The subject's bone-white hair, cast against a shadowy background, clearly identified her.

I let the drawings slip from my hands and suddenly felt queasy as I realized I hadn't stumbled on an artist's studio but a well-used lover's den. Julie may have preferred Eastern spiritualism for her coaching sessions, but when it came to lustful encounters with an employee, she was all Middle East.

I was so distracted by the drawings that I didn't notice the dark lump nestled in the pillows along the far wall. My eyes strained to see into the part of the room that was so dimly lit from the outside. I slowly approached and pulled back one of the giant pillows and found a man slumped face down on the cushion. There was something sticky on the pillow I was holding, and I realized too late that it was his blood, masked perfectly by the pillow's burgundy shade. I dropped the pillow and stared at my crimson-stained hand.

"YOU!" a voice shouted behind me, so startling that I lurched upward and cracked my head on the rock overhang. There was that moment when I was fully aware of the pain about to come but for a blissful half-second I felt nothing. I reached up to touch my skull and comfort the impending throbbing.

The voice didn't like that.

"Don't you move!" it shouted. "Get down on the ground."

A second voice repeated the same instruction but with a few expletives thrown in. I surmised from the excessive shouting that they were cops.

"Look, fellas, this area...it's a little dirty," I said, and tried to back up without provoking them. "If I could just step out here—"

It seemed they didn't need much prodding because I was immediately bull-rushed and tackled to the floor.

The Turkish throw pillows were soft but the million-year-old boulder wasn't. For the second time in the span of thirty seconds my head cracked on the stone. I lay face down in the cushions as what felt like a dozen sets of knees tried to prove how flexible a human spine can be. One of those knees found the back of my neck and pressed my face further into the cushions.

I didn't know what was more unnerving—the fact that my face was buried in pillows from a crime scene or that it was in pillows that Julie St. Jean had used in her elaborate lovemaking sessions.

After being frisked and having my pockets emptied of belongings, I was led out in handcuffs to an idling cruiser in the street. The excitement drew all the neighbors out of their warm houses and into the rain. The inhabitants of Sierra Madre were more of a mackinaw-and-rain-slicker crowd than golf-umbrella types.

I scanned the sea of red and yellow coats but didn't spot Rebecca. I did, however, see the counterman from the coffee shop. Still wearing his apron, he had the smirk on his face of someone who'd just served a cold slice of justice. I assumed he was the one who'd called the cops.

"Asshole," I mouthed through the cruiser window.

The bastard winked back at me.

With so many spectators in such a tight space and no room for residents to get by, the police made the decision to move me to the local station. And although I had done almost nothing wrong and didn't even know the people staring at me, I couldn't help but feel some level of humiliation. What made it worse was that the officer had to execute a fifty-plus-point turn to get the cruiser pointed back toward the bottom of the hill. Navigating the narrow streets was apparently a local pastime because everyone got in on the act, calling out instructions, giving hand signals, and generally laughing at the officer's ineptitude behind the wheel.

Everyone had an opinion, except for one person standing away from the crowd, not quite hidden but not wanting to be seen either. It appeared to be a little old man in a baseball cap and a black jacket that was a raincoat in name only as it didn't look like it could shed much water.

As the officer finally cleared his front bumper, he headed the car down the hill. We passed the old man, who quickly angled his face away from us. I turned to watch the figure disappear between a set of homes like someone very familiar with the area.

Julie St. Jean still knew her old neighborhood.

A TOUCH OF HEARTH

W hat took you so long?" Rebecca asked as I walked out of the Sierra Madre police station.

"Some chatty rookie detective," I said, pretending to be annoyed. What legitimately annoyed me was the five hundred bucks I needlessly agreed to pay on a trespassing charge.

Despite what my attorney ex-wife ingrained in me during years of her shouting at the TV while we watched true-crime shows together, I declined the offer to obtain legal representation. Lawyers do one thing really well—they keep you from talking. But this time I wanted to talk, not so much to provide information to the police but to see what kind of information they had for me. I was operating in the dark and clamming up would only keep me from gaining clarity on what Julie was up to.

But the questions I asked and the vague responses I gave to their questions succeeded only in raising their suspicions about me. Suddenly I found myself having to document my whereabouts over the last week, which then had to be confirmed. I wasn't released until later that evening.

I welcomed the cold air after so long in the infinitely recycled air inside the police station. The rain clouds were finally clearing and the moon shone through in a crispness that arrives only after many days of rain. Rebecca looked paler than normal in that light.

"Have you been out here the entire time?" I asked.

"No, I hung around the house up there. Spoke to some of the neighbors and police officers. They gave me a lift over here."

"You should have just gone home," I said.

"I have no home and you have all my stuff in the back of your car."

My ineptitude at pumping information from the police left this poor woman with nowhere to go. I quickly ordered a car to take us back to the coffee shop to collect my car, and then we made the short jaunt down to my home in Eagle Rock.

"I got some good information out of the police," I said on the drive. "A little bit on the dead man."

"Long way from Bakersfield," Rebecca replied cryptically.

"What's that?"

"Fitch," she said. "He's a long way from home."

I nodded as if I already knew this, but it was new information to me.

"Fitch?" I repeated, as I recalled where I'd heard that

name before. "That's the name the man in the hotel was asking about."

"I know," she said.

"That's who was killed?"

"Didn't the police tell you?" she asked, confused.

"No, they didn't go into that much detail."

"You were there for four hours," she said.

I felt the need to justify why my interviewing skills got me less information than Rebecca had gathered in one-fifth the time.

"We were exploring other avenues," I said.

"They told you about the money, right?" she asked.

I was clearly in the dark. It felt like one of those conference calls where someone asks you a direct question but you can't answer it because you weren't listening. Asking them to repeat the question is an admission that you weren't paying attention. The trick is to ask a question back without tipping your hand that you've been staring out the window the entire time.

"I want to make sure we're talking about the same thing," I told her. "What did they tell you about the money?"

"I imagine the same thing they told you." Rebecca wasn't playing along.

"Maybe," I tried again. "But I'm curious to hear how they positioned it."

"Huh?"

"Just to see if it lines up with what my guy told me."

"They told you about it, right?"

I started to feel like I was on that conference call

again. Everyone pretends like nothing happened, but you can hear the shame in their voices. The only recourse is to turn on the questioner to get the heat off of oneself.

"How can you be sure the people you spoke to have the right information?" I challenged.

"It's the same people who spoke to you, I think."

Mercifully, she finally shared what information she had gotten from the arresting officer and lead detective. Fitch was holding a check for a hundred thousand dollars, made out to him by Lois Hearns. The police wanted to know if Rebecca knew anything about it, but all of these developments were new to her. In their questioning they gave up more information than they got out of her.

I tried to play it off like the information she had was nothing new to me.

"That's pretty much what they told me," I confirmed, but inside I silently cursed the cops. They kept me in a room for four hours and told me zilch, but then all but opened the case file with Rebecca.

We stopped off at my house before heading downtown to check Rebecca into her new hotel. The place was cold by Los Angeles standards. Anything below sixty-five degrees warranted a fire, so I placed more logs than were needed onto the grate and lit it from below with the gas burners. It was roaring in a matter of minutes. There was a lot to discuss and a nice fire felt like a good accompaniment as we tried to make sense of all that we had learned that day.

But as I dragged a chair over to be closer to the hearth, Rebecca remained seated on the edge of the couch across the room. She didn't look like someone who wanted to talk. If anything, the way she sat forward on the couch made it seem like she was about to leave.

Every topic I threw out—the used-car purchase, the money paid to Fitch, the Sierra Madre home itself—was greeted with less interest than the previous one until we reached a point where Rebecca simply stood up and announced that she was taking off.

"Where are you going?" I asked.

"I don't know, I'll probably just head home. Don't worry about driving me," she said, "I'll call a car. I'll just need to get my stuff out of yours."

"The way you say it sounds like this is it. What's going on?"

"Nothing," she said. "I was just thinking about it while waiting for you outside the precinct and decided it isn't fair. You didn't sign up for this," she gestured with her hand at the night outside, in an attempt to convey two murders and someone on the run, all beyond the glass. "You were nice enough to offer to help me, and I'm really grateful. But this wasn't a part of the bargain and I need to respect that."

"Okay," I said. "Maybe you're right." But I couldn't mask my disappointment. After a long day during which we learned many things, it seemed odd to just call it quits like this. Despite my bumbling with the Sierra Madre police, I was able to uncover some important information to help this woman, who by any stretch of the imagination could use it. She was sick, alone, and in search of answers. And now that we'd found a couple of clues, she wanted to give up.

"Just so you know," I started, "one thing I've learned over the years is that anytime you ask someone what's wrong and their first reply is 'nothing,' whatever comes next is complete bullshit."

Rebecca studied me but made no protest.

"I saw Julie," I told her.

"You did? Where?"

"The same place you saw her," I answered.

I had purposely withheld the detail about spotting Julie at the crime scene. Ever since the discovery of the tray of pills in her room, I began to tread lightly around Rebecca out of a fear of unnecessarily upsetting her. But illness or not, Rebecca was still human.

"I think you hung around here because you wanted to know if I had seen her. Well, I did." I let that hang out there because with this new piece of information, there were many more questions to be answered. She couldn't leave now. "You probably want to know what I told the police."

She looked up expectantly.

"I didn't tell them anything."

Rebecca stared into the fire. I wanted to think it was a subtle act of contrition but I couldn't be sure.

"Were you going to tell me?" I asked.

"No," she answered.

"How come?"

"I don't know."

"Are you supposed to meet Julie somewhere?" I asked. "I'm not a lawyer—but that's probably a bad idea. It makes you complicit in some serious stuff. But whatever, you know what you're doing. I don't need to tell you what to do."

Rebecca let me ramble on and then had a question of her own.

"Why do you want to help me?"

"Good question," I said, the classic corporate response to a question when you don't know the answer. I used the delay to try to think of one but came up empty. "I don't know why."

Rebecca seemed to accept my lack of a reason.

"The bank in Pasadena," she said after a few moments. "The one on the GPS from the loaner car?"

"You did know about it," I answered for her.

"A few months back, I found a checkbook in Julie's things. There were a few records of payments...to Lois," she finished. In a tone that tried to convey the degree of her disappointment, she added, "It was for a lot of money."

"How much?"

"Three payments. Two hundred thousand each."

"Did you ask her about it?"

I assumed that the discovery of the checkbook in "Julie's things" meant an element of snooping on the part of a suspicious spouse. Confronting a loved one about that discovery often got the issue thrown back in your face for one's lack of faith.

"I brought it up once," Rebecca answered. "She

dismissed it as nothing to fret over. 'An insignificant blip.'" After a moment's reflection she added, "That's Julie for you."

They were the lighthearted words of someone rationalizing the faults of the person they love.

I quickly processed the latest developments in my head—a bank account that Julie kept secret from Rebecca, a love nest that she also kept from her partner, several checks made out to her lover for a sizable amount of money. It all pointed to a single conclusion, one that I was reluctant to bring up directly with Rebecca.

"Who handles the finances for Power of One?" I asked, although I thought I knew the answer. When it came time to pay, you got the call from Rebecca, not Julie. The guru delivered the inspirational messages but collecting the money was an unsavory task left for the minions. "Could Lois have been skimming money off the top?"

"I handle the money for the firm," Rebecca stated. "And our books are in order."

The second part of her answer headed off my next question, which would have been to inquire if Julie could be dipping into her own firm. It happens when people get into financial binds; sometimes the only answer is to steal from themselves.

"Do you and Julie combine finances?" I asked.

"I assume by that question you want to know if we have separate bank accounts?" she retorted. "No, we share everything. And since I didn't know about this one in Pasadena, you want to know why I think she felt the need to have one?" Rebecca was clearly getting frustrated. "You corporate guys just talk in circles all day. Can't someone just be direct, for once?" The question was addressed to more than just me.

"What am I talking around?"

"The fact that my wife and Lois were having an affair," she said flatly. "Clearly you knew this also."

Now it was my turn to feel guilty for holding back information.

"I think they were using the Sierra Madre home to see each other."

"You *think* they were?" she chided me again.

"They *were* using the home for their affair," I corrected. My directness was oddly appreciated by Rebecca. She even thanked me for it. "Was Lois blackmailing her?"

"I don't know," she said. "Somehow I don't see Julie ever feeling the need to pay someone to keep something like that a secret."

I sifted through her words to find the unstated meaning behind them.

"Was there some sort of arrangement between you two?"

"An arrangement to feel jilted?" she replied, laughing bitterly. "No, I didn't sign up for that." After a short pause she again said, "That's Julie for you."

It was the second time she'd used that phrase, but in this instance it didn't feel like a way to excuse someone's sins. It felt more like someone's reluctant acceptance of them. "Well, you finally got your backstory," she said, sounding both embarrassed and relieved. She pulled a chair over and sat in front of the fire.

We let the intermittent pops from the burning logs fill the silence. After a while I took up the poker and made a few adjustments and then we started talking. We spoke about a lot of things, including childhood fireplaces that only got lit on Christmas, and the blue-flame variety that was environmentally conscious but an insult to the word fire. One thing we didn't talk about was Julie. After almost two decades of working together on bogus seminars and human-engagement programs, when we sometimes spent multi-week sessions in each other's company with mandatory cocktail hours and dinners every night, it took just one full day of looking for an estranged spouse for Rebecca and me to finally have an authentic discussion.

At some point I suggested she crash in my spare bedroom. Rebecca didn't flinch when I made the offer and didn't run when she saw the actual room, which was more a walk-in closet by today's standards, with just enough room for a twin bed and a cheap nightstand.

"It's perfect," she said, but judging by the look on her face, a pile of hay covered in burlap would have garnered the same response. Exhaustion overrode any misgivings over a twin bed with scratchy sheets and that unique kind of loneliness that only a spare bedroom can have.

"Let's talk in the morning," she said as I closed the door behind me. It was her way of confirming that she still needed my help to find Julie.

A SHADE OF AMBER

Badger didn't believe in writing things down.

Whereas the corporate world memorialized everything from sneezes to bathroom visits in a PowerPoint deck, he preferred the old-fashioned verbal approach. If you were lucky enough to get something down on paper from him, it was likely on the back of an overdue bill notice.

"She's ass out," he told me.

Badger and I were at the café outside my building. Sensing this was a non–firm-related meeting, he spared me the dank suit and opted for his traditional attire of tight jeans, an even tighter sweater, and amber-tinted sunglasses.

"Julie?" I asked. "How bad?"

"Piss broke," he continued. "Got a stack of liens on the business, underwater on the PV house, and getting sued up the wazoo: the building management company for breach of contract, that company in Culver for false representation pertaining to the sale of a business, a printer in Bell Gardens for non-payment—"

"Wait," I interrupted, "what company in Culver City?"

"The one you guys were talking about," he answered. "Color-Whatever-the-Hell-They-Call-Themselves."

"Nalysis," I filled in for him. "What did you mean by sale of a business? Who sold what to whom?"

Badger explained that ColorNalysis had bought the rights to Power of One's intellectual property but had then pulled out due to misrepresentation of terms.

I smiled at the idea of buying someone else's gibberish and then suing them because there was nothing in the box when you finally got it. The smile faded when I started to wonder why I was hearing this from Badger and not the woman staying in my house.

"The murdered woman did the deal," he added.

"Lois Hearns? She was a lawyer?"

"A bad one, it sounds like. She hasn't been practicing for years but her name is on all the deal documents."

Badger had uncovered a significant amount of information in a very short time and it showed on his face. He looked very proud of himself. Now it was my turn to impress.

"Julie's been making payments to Lois for several months. Probably too large for her legal services but they have to be connected to what's going on."

"Maybe," he said tersely.

I then recounted the discovery of the lover's den in

Sierra Madre, Fitch's body among its pillows, and the secret bank account in Pasadena. With each new detail I divulged, Badger grew more sullen. It was as if any new information that didn't source directly from him besmirched his reputation as a top-flight investigator. Badger was at his best with constant ego stroking, so I returned to a field in which we could both be proud of his accomplishments.

"How's it all connect?" I asked.

"It's your classic lesbo-affair/blackmail-the-cheating-spouse routine," he said, seeming slightly annoyed that he even had to spell it out for me. "This Fitch guy does the strong-arming. Your 'boy' doesn't like it and fights back. Two people end up dead."

"Blackmail, huh?" I repeated, and pretended to process it. I must have oversold it because he grew sullen again.

"Just like you suspected," he said.

"Badger—"

But he held up his hand to stop me.

"Sorry," I said. "I initially thought of the blackmail angle but dismissed it after talking with Rebecca. It still could be a shakedown but not over the affair."

Badger nodded.

"I won't charge you for the work," he said. And to prove how sincere he was, he added, "I have standards, you know."

Naturally, I didn't believe him. Private investigation wasn't the most lucrative of trades, and turning down a job could equate to him not eating for a week.

"I appreciate you offering," I told him, but left off whether or not I was going to accept it.

He got a little nervous that he might have overplayed his hand and supplied some more information in order to prove he did indeed deserve payment.

"Julie might be broke," he began casually, "but she could always fall back on her old job."

"Which was?"

"Librarian."

"Is that a joke?"

"Badger doesn't tell jokes when he's working," he admonished.

I continued laughing anyway. I could think of a thousand other jobs for Julie before ever coming up with that one.

"There's no way."

"Believe it."

Julie had worked at the Sierra Madre Library for nearly a decade before leaving in the early 1980s. Badger didn't have an employment record for her until several years later when she established Power of One.

I shook my head at the thought of this woman going from working a small-town card catalogue to coaching executives in the boardroom. Of the countless reinvention stories that make up Los Angeles, this had to be one of the better ones.

Badger slid a Santa Anita betting slip across the table.

"You're giving me one of your losers from the track?"

"Turn it over," he instructed.

Written on the back was a phone number and address in Burbank.

"The murdered woman's contact info in case you wanted to talk to her husband," Badger said. "I thought you would."

Once again I was legitimately impressed with his ability to find out so much information in such a short span of time.

Apparently Badger was also impressed with himself because he took off his sunglasses so I could look him directly in the eyes. It was an unnecessary gesture given that I could already clearly see them through the amber lenses.

"You, my friend, have an itch." He rose dramatically from the table. "And Badger needs to help you scratch it."

I would have chosen another visual but I was grateful for the sentiment. Before I could thank him, Badger strode off with the swagger of a man who knew he was going to get paid.

"It's what I do," he shouted loud enough for everyone in the café to recognize his oversized dedication.

SANCTUARY

A flooded water main near Griffith Park ruined what had up until then been a successful shortcut into the Valley. The storm drains couldn't handle the volume of water coming down off Los Feliz and traffic backed up all the way along Riverside Drive. By the time I made it to Lois Hearns's home in Burbank it was well past dark.

Her street's best feature was that it was an effective shortcut between two of the big studios. Otherwise it was an unkempt stretch lined with ficus trees decades past the point of needing pruning. The house was a substandard ranch that hadn't been updated since the 1950s. A few of the shutters leaned against the garage as if begging for someone to return them to their rightful home. It looked like they had been waiting for a while.

I walked up the short driveway and approached the attached garage. The door was partly ajar, and I could see the glare of a fluorescent light inside as well as a pair of work boots moving around. I called out to announce my presence but didn't get a response. I knocked on the cheap aluminum door, which rattled more loudly than I needed it to.

"Yeah?" barked a voice.

I didn't get very far into my planned introduction.

"I'm busy," came the response.

"I'll try not to take up too much of your time," I said, and then added a little tidbit to whet his appetite. "It's about the money."

"It's always about the money," I heard him say, and then watched a hand curl under the door and shove it high up on its rails. I stepped inside but he didn't lower the door behind me. Maybe he anticipated my visit would be short.

The walls were lined with well-marked work-shelves and covered in pegboard holding more types of wrenches than I thought existed. A few red tool chests on caster wheels served as hubs of the work activity. At the center sat an old engine from some hot rod long past its racing days perched on a block like a lion statue. A portable infrared heater chased out some of the cold, damp air, and although I was loath to get any grease on my work slacks, this place just begged for me to pull up a stool, crack a beer, and talk about engine parts that I knew nothing about.

"I'm always interested in money," he said with a smile, "as long as it isn't the kind leaving my wallet."

"We're of like minds," I told him.

He shot me a look.

"Maybe."

Mr. Hearns was in his sixties. He wore tired jeans and a paper-thin white T-shirt from which a pair of long arms hung like ropes. Two golf balls under the skin served as elbows. His yellow-gray hair was pulled back into a ponytail, but I wasn't about to resent him for it. Where my co-worker Paul wore his as a symbol of some insincere allegiance to the counterculture, Hearns's fit with his legitimate toughness. He looked like someone with deceptive strength, the kind that you discovered too late.

"First, let me offer my condolences," I started. "A tragic development, to say the least."

"Yes, it was," he replied. "We had the service today."

"I wasn't aware," I said. "Apologies for intruding."

Hearns was a difficult man to read. I couldn't tell if he was upset or indifferent or something else. After a moment, it was clear he wasn't ready to shoo me away just yet.

"So did Lo have some kind of insurance policy or something?"

"Not that I know of," I said, and then wondered why he immediately shot to this potential money source presented to him by a perfect stranger. He gave me his reason, which came in the form of an insult.

"You look like an insurance man," he said, shrugging.

I had hoped to present myself as some sort of detective of the official or private kind. Having been dismissed as a hawker of extended warranties, I now had to defend the significance of an imaginary role.

"Trust me, I am not in insurance," I scoffed. "I help people recover money, like the large payments made to your wife over the last year."

"Cops said something about that," he said.

"Did you know about it?" I asked.

"Not until they told me. Bastards thought I had it." After giving it some proper reflection, he added, "Man, I hate cops."

"Everyone does."

Our mutual distaste for law enforcement put me right in his book.

"So large sums, huh?"

He was trying to coax out what different interpretations he and I might have of the word *large*.

"Couple hundred thousand," I told him.

He whistled between the gap in his front teeth. His gaze fell on me with the glare reserved for job candidates. His posture got a little stiffer. I knew where this was headed.

"And where do you fit in?" he asked. "You a lawyer?"

He said the last word with the same vitriol he'd used to express his views on law enforcement.

"Lo was a lawyer," he added, then said, as if sensing my confusion, "before she got into the art thing."

"Well, I'm not a lawyer," I said. "But we can help you recover the money."

"Who's 'we' and how much do you charge for this so-called service?"

I made up a firm using my surname and the street I grew up on and then added "Associates" at the end to make it sound more legitimate.

"We take a third," I explained.

Hearns didn't look like someone who got fast ones pulled on him very often. And if he did, the perpetrator might end up regretting it. But I reasoned that lawyers take a third—at least that's what legal dramas say—and that amount felt right. I didn't want to get into the specifics of what exactly my firm did because I didn't have a clue.

"That's a big chunk. I could always get it myself," he said.

"Maybe."

"You know, we never officially got divorced," he added, which was his way of asking me to confirm that he had a right to that money.

I didn't oblige and simply nodded my head. I found that men like Mr. Hearns often had a deep insecurity around educated men. Their antagonism masked a disabling inferiority complex. It also made them surprisingly compliant.

"Who am I kidding," he said, laughing. "Lois handled all the finances. Seventy percent of nothing is still nothing."

"Sixty-six percent," I corrected, and extended my hand. "We got a deal?"

He might as well have put my hand in his workshop's vice, as I felt my knuckles fold over in his grip. But he then showed mercy by placing a very cold can of beer in my aching hand, pulled from the beat-up fridge on the far wall. I finally got my wish to crack a cold one—but we weren't two old buds talking manifolds. We spoke instead about the topic men never talk about.

"I'd like to ask you some questions about your wife but want to be respectful…"

"Ex-wife," he interrupted. "We've been separated for years," he said with a wave of his hand, the sort of response someone gave who had fallen out of love a long time before. It was also the response of someone mortally wounded from loss who didn't want to admit it. I let silence flush out which one it was.

"She developed a taste for tuna later in life," he said, and then I knew my answer and just how painful the event had been to him. He had the bitterness of a spurned man, but it was the particularly acrid kind when that other someone isn't a man but another woman.

"I know about the affair," I said.

"You know about that old bag?" he said, which I assumed referenced Julie St. Jean.

"Yes, she's the source of the potential money. How long had it been going on?"

"God only knows. A while."

"You've met her?"

"I went to a party at her house once. Wasn't for me—too much cheese and wine and craft-beer bullshit," he answered. "Maybe Lois fell for the money, the lifestyle."

The warm and inviting garage suddenly lost some of its charm.

"What kind of money did Lois make working for Power of One?"

"I don't know what she made," he said. "Lo handled

all the finances…we never talked money."

It was the second time he had said that.

"Did you still live together after you were separated? Establishing cohabitation, even legally separated, will help your cause."

"Yeah, she never really left. She'd be gone for days, sometimes weeks. Then show back up. Just something we kind of worked out together."

It didn't sound like Hearns had a say in that agreement. I saw a man accepting of any deal that didn't involve a clean break. At least that way there was always a chance, however slim, of rekindling what was long past snuffed out.

"But she lived here, no question about that. I got bills that can prove it," he said, and made a move to go get them.

"It's okay," I tried, but Hearns ignored me.

I followed him out of the garage and into the front of his house. The living room was trimly decorated with a certain unclassifiable style. It was part tribal and part Americana.

"Nice place," I said.

"Lo was the decorator," he said, and shrugged like he didn't much care for the decorations or decorating in general, but there was a vein of pride in his words.

Hearns led me into the kitchen, propped a large accordion file on the table, and riffled through the contents. While he searched for the documents, I spotted an unopened phone bill on the table.

"I got a gas bill with her name on it," he said, hand-ing me a bill notice. "Here's water and sanitation," he added as he shoved another my way.

"This should be sufficient," I told him.

As we made our way to the door, I tucked the documents under my coat to keep them from getting wet. The rain was starting again and I thought about the quick run back to my car.

"Thanks for the beer," I said, stepping down into the rain. "I'll be in touch."

"You know the cops thought I killed her," he proffered. I turned to look back at him. Hearns stared out at the darkness like he had forgotten I was there. "How could they ever think that?" His voice quavered.

I left him there in the doorway and went back to my car. I drove past several houses, then pulled into an open space and got out in the rain. For a guy who didn't know anything about the couple's finances, he certainly kept very thorough records of them. I headed back toward the house.

I could see his work boots shuffling about through the opening in the garage door. I quietly moved past it toward the front entrance. The screen door was stuck and I had to give a gentle yank. The clatter of the rain masked whatever sounds I made. With one eye on the garage, I stepped into the house and fumbled in the dark toward the kitchen table.

The accordion file was still there. The unopened phone bill lay next to it on the table. If the couple hadn't made a clean break, as Hearns had stated, then the phone bill would contain a log of calls made both by him and his ex-wife—very valuable information when trying to piece together the timeline leading up to Lois's murder.

I slipped the envelope into my coat and headed back out.

Passing the garage again, I no longer saw the work boots and my stomach churned at the thought of a confrontation with Hearns. I didn't think I could outrun him in the rain wearing loafers.

I stepped over a river of water pouring from a downspout and passed a small window permanently covered by a cheap, plastic blind. Through one of the missing slats I spied Hearns leaning against his workbench, his eyes fixed on the floor, and his hand wrapped around another can of beer. He took a long pull, long enough to finish the entire thing. But whatever he hoped for it to do, it didn't succeed. He shook his head hopelessly and moved toward the old fridge.

He had the look of someone determined to get drunk. I felt a pang of guilt for intruding on whatever nightly routine he carried out in the quiet of his sanctuary. I slowly stepped back but kept an eye on the slat just in case he caught the movement outside.

I stopped.

Hearns was at the fridge but he didn't pull out another can of beer. Instead, he opened the freezer, moved aside some blocks of frozen steaks, and pulled a thin package wrapped in plastic from the back. I couldn't see exactly what it was because he had his back to me. But I watched him unwrap it and discard the plastic.

Then I watched him shove a sheaf of large bills into his jeans' back pocket.

MAP MY CHROMA

nsightful leaders inspiring change."

"What's that?" I asked as I racked my brain, trying to remember where I had heard that line before.

"How can I help you reach that next level?" she replied.

"I'm sorry," I said, "but which number did I call?"

"This is ColorNalysis," she answered.

I quickly checked the phone records I'd gotten from the murdered woman's husband. I had assigned various highlighters to the regular numbers on the bill and colored them in. The bill quickly resembled a landscape watercolor. Julie's baby blue entries were of such large proportion they made the sky seem endless. There was a little green that was as rare as the calls were short—those were to her husband. And then there were these sporadic but lengthy rows of orange that indicated calls to ColorNalysis, Power of One's rival consulting firm.

I told the woman on the phone I was interested in coming in and meeting with them to talk about what they had to offer. The bubbly voice confidently announced they had the solution to my problem, even though I never said what the problem was or that I had one in the first place. I was given an appointment for later that morning.

Their office was a three-room space in the downtown section of Culver City. The small lobby sported a nice view of the old hotel and movie theater. As could be expected with outfits like these, they projected a young, hip image with their interior design of clean lines and almost monastic décor. Consultants were in a relentless pursuit of relevance and nothing undermined that more than that euphemism for old age, *stodgy*.

For that reason I was momentarily perplexed by the physical representation of the effervescent voice I'd spoken to that morning. While she was clearly under thirty, there was something slightly anachronistic about her ensemble: a gray suit, conservative black shoes, and dark hair pulled tightly into a barrette. It was overly old-fashioned and didn't seem to fit, but once I met her boss I fully understood her role at the firm—to contrast with the "youth" of the founder.

Bronson Thibideux sat somewhere around the half-century mark but did everything he could to defy his age. You could say it was the clothes—jeans and flip-flops—or his casual demeanor—always a "hey man" and often a few curse words—but there was also something deeper inside him that just made you feel old in his presence. As I watched him from across the acrylic conference table, I couldn't help but think Power of One didn't stand a chance.

"What an insane development," he said, referencing the events of the last week. "Blew our minds when we heard the news."

The collective pronoun reflected the firm, not necessarily the old-young woman sitting next to him, although she nodded in agreement.

"Do you know Julie St. Jean personally?" I asked.

"We go way back," he replied. "A good egg if there ever was one." I reflected that she had to be a little rotten, wanted as she was for two murders. "I don't even know how we can talk business after all that's gone down," he intoned, but then proceeded to do just that. "Thanks for reaching out. You guys have been on our radar for years as a company that could benefit from a partnership with ColorNalysis."

At least Bronson had more decorum than some of his counterparts in the industry. He allowed a short grace period before aggressively calling for my business. Others weren't so respectful; I had gotten three requests to meet from other consultants in the last two days. Blood was in the water surrounding Power of One, and the feeding frenzy to carve up their client base was about to begin. This worked for me, as Bronson believed I was there to learn about his services, when what I really wanted to know was why he had so many conversations with Lois Hearns in the days leading up to her murder.

Bronson caught me looking at the laminated cop-
ies of their Chroma-Maps perched on mini-easels on
the table.

"This is powerful stuff," he told me, holding the
color card. "It saved my marriage."

Your third one, I wanted to clarify, but bit my tongue.

"Chuck, it's about embracing the individual," he explained, and I nodded for no real reason. "We tend to
put people into categories—the do-gooder, the procras-
tinator, the hard-charger—but the reality is, and something that has been borne out in science, mind you, is
that this is all a human fabrication. We are not just one
kind of person. We are many kinds of infinite combi-
nations. And once you acknowledge that, embrace it,
even, then you will see the power of mindful interac-
tions. That's what these are for," he said, pointing to the
card with blobs of colors on it. "It's about giving full
transparency to who we are as individuals so that as a
team we can better operate in the collective unit."

During his spiel, I realized the woman by his side
had another role besides making her boss look younger.
It was to listen to Bronson as if he was unveiling some
truth that had for centuries been hidden in a shroud
of secrecy. She had this annoying habit of periodically
pulling her gaze from her boss so she could stare at me
with a look that shouted, "Amazing, right?"

But none of it was amazing. It was the same pab-
lum dished out by all these types of consultants. They
latched onto some "fresh" idea and constructed a belief
system around it that would somehow elevate team dy-

namics, collaboration, productivity…whatever was the buzzword of the day.

I didn't begrudge them their desire to make a buck—they could spew nonsense to their heart's content—but that didn't mean I had to be impressed by it. After the third time the young woman turned to me to confirm my awe, I crossed my arms over my chest and shook my head like a disgruntled Soviet commissar.

"How does your program differentiate itself from Power of One?" I asked, breaking into the monologue to explore a topic in which I was more interested.

"Look, they've done some amazing things," he said. The past tense was intentional and didn't go unnoticed.

"But they've lost a step?" I filled in for him.

"It's not for me to comment," he said, laughing. "Especially given the current circumstances. But you could say they are…entering a necessary period of innovation."

It was the most serious of accusations: Power of One had grown stale.

"They've been using a new member, a sort of Visioning Artist who captures the mood of brainstorming sessions," I said. "It's highly effective."

"I've heard of others doing that," he said dismissively.

"She's real good," I continued. "Lois something. Lois Hearns? You know her?"

Bronson shook his head, while still appearing to scour his memory for some recollection of the name.

"Tragically, she was the one murdered in Julie's home," I added, trying to help dust off some of those convenient cobwebs.

"Nope, doesn't ring a bell." He turned to his lackey. "Have you...?"

"No," she spouted. "I'm not really familiar with that name."

"Let me ask you something," Bronson said to me. "Are you happy with the outcomes you are getting with Power of One?"

"If I knew what they were actually trying to achieve then maybe I could answer your question."

Bronson leaned back in his chair and studied me with a wry look, then turned to the young woman.

"He's so cyan," he said to her.

"I know, right?" she agreed, all smiles.

Bronson gave a self-satisfied chuckle and his flunkey laughed a lot harder once she saw the boss had deemed it appropriate. That's when I noticed they had another set of Chroma-Maps in front of them—an identical pair that I assumed charted *my* "unique" personality.

Many years back when their firm was bidding for a contract with mine, they demonstrated their system with live reads on me and a few others who were evaluating their capabilities. Seeing they still had my map was like discovering your Stasi file after the Wall came down. I felt oddly exposed but also angry. And the fact that they were now structuring their discussion with insights from my map only further infuriated me.

"What exactly does *cyan* mean?" I asked.

Having taken the bait, Bronson effortlessly transitioned into the pitch.

"It's your dominant color," he explained. Cyan encompassed the qualities of someone who took a singular focus in life, who got validation from tangible accomplishments, and who grew frustrated with ambiguity. Those who used this quality well were most likely highly effective leaders of diverse groups of individuals. Their value was not always fully recognized but their influence was substantial.

As he rattled on like this for several minutes, I found myself nodding because I could see myself in his description of cyan. I *was* a good leader. I *was* effective. And goddammit, I deserved that recognition! It took another "amazing, right?" look from the acolyte to bring me back to reality. I then rode out the rest of his speech in a slightly sickened state from having temporarily fallen for it. I always took pride in being able to see through the nonsense, but here I had briefly fallen for Bronson's flavor of it.

The Chroma-Map was simply a more elaborate version of the cards a fortune teller uses to see into your soul. They worked because you made them work. You filled in the holes, you validated the vague declarations. The "science" of the brain mapping that supposedly led to those discoveries was no different than the incense in the card reader's room—it was layered on to make it feel legitimate.

The Chroma-Map's power was in convincing someone they were unique. And despite Bronson's claim that we are all individuals, the part he overlooked was that in at least one way we are all very much the same— we all want to believe in something.

I told Bronson that I was interested in learning more about a potential future partnership. Naturally, I had no interest in his claptrap program but I was interested in why he lied about knowing Lois. I felt I could string him along with the promise of a big payday while I figured it out. I threw him a bone and mentioned that some of our employees were familiar with his work and spoke highly of it, including someone in my HR group.

"I know Paul well," he said, smiling. "You've got a good one there." As measured by the amount of money he funneled into ColorNalysis, I assumed. "We pair up well. Very compatible colors. If I may suggest, why don't Paul and I team up on this? We'll be able to do some good work together."

"I'm sure you would," I said, "but I'd prefer you and I work on this together as we explore how 'compatible' our colors are."

That seemed to take a little of the air out of the room.

"I look forward to it," Bronson muttered, his own color suddenly turning a little gray.

POOR FITCHIE

old it to Bronson?" repeated Rebecca. Her tone spoke of admiration for Julie's ability to pull a fast one on Bronson, on her, or perhaps on both of them.

"I take it the business isn't worth much?" I asked.

"Double whatever number is in your head and that's how much we owe." Rebecca caught herself. "I shouldn't be so dismissive. It was always 'Julie's company,' but I had a certain pride in helping to build it...."

"Even if you never got any credit for it," I finished for her.

"I had to give up the day-to-day running once I got sick," she said, then let out a small laugh. "I knew Julie couldn't handle it on her own, but I never thought she'd run it into the ground!"

"Lois helped. You know she was a lawyer?"

"I didn't know that."

"And in contact with ColorNalysis."

"What else did the phone records say?" She politely waited out my silence and added, "You can tell me."

In the hours leading up to her murder, I related, Lois had called Julie many times. The calls rose to a frenzied level, with dozens placed no more than a minute apart, until they abruptly stopped, as it turned out, forever. It confirmed that Julie was in contact with Lois almost to the moment of her death. What else it meant was up to the person receiving this information.

Rebecca just nodded but withheld comment.

I pulled my eyes from the road and studied her out of the corner of my eye. We had just come from another treatment and she didn't look well at all. Her movements were slow and pained. Her breaths were like those of a neglected aquarium fish trying to work a forever-insufficient amount of oxygenated water through its gills.

I began to regret allowing her to come on the trip to Bakersfield. Badger had gotten me the address for James Fitch, the murdered man in the Sierra Madre house. I thought I might learn a little more about him and his connection to Julie. But it was a ways from Los Angeles, one long rise and fall over a four-thousand-foot hump known as the Tehachapi Mountains, and Rebecca didn't look up for it.

"Stop," she said, her eyes closed and head resting against the passenger window.

"Stop what?"

"Looking at me. I'll be fine."

I was prone, just like everyone else, to revert to the emotional clichés reserved for the sick—equal parts pity for their suffering and admiration for their courage. That usually manifested itself in hollow statements about a "brave fight" or some other pugilistic reference. Rebecca had made it clear early on that that kind of talk was both unwarranted and unwanted: "There's nothing brave about wanting to stay alive."

This last statement revived a memory of my father's end with the disease. He chose to fight it but it wasn't much of a battle. If anything, he was just some guy waiting for the referee to stop the fight.

I let her sleep on the long drive into the San Joaquin Valley. The I-5 was a major route for semis bringing crap from China north and fresh produce south. The result was a challenging drive with big rigs lugging tons of cargo up a hill at thirty miles an hour while anyone with a V8 blew by them going eighty. My sensible sedan nestled in behind one of the rigs like a pilot fish finding safety among a pod of migrating blue whales. Two attempts to venture into the dark waters of the passing lane sent me scurrying back when pickups appeared in my mirror with flashes of high beams signaling me to get out of the way, quickly.

We crested the summit with the dying sun filtering through ominous rain clouds. Signs warned of dangerous driving conditions and reminded drivers to use headlights and to not venture further unless one's trunk contained snow chains. I ignored these warnings and left the safety of a pod of semis to glide down the long

grade through the Tejon Pass, past the handful of run-
away truck ramps and farther into the Grapevine until we finally hit the bed of the San Joaquin Valley and
cruised our way toward Bakersfield.

Rosedale Village RV Park sat on the far edge of town
and featured a stunning view of nothing. I marveled at
the vastness of a landscape so perfectly flat that even
a steamroller couldn't achieve that level of perfection.
Scanning the area, I suppressed the urge to ponder just
why anyone would want to live here because the second part of that question contained the answer—*if you
didn't have to.*

I drove through the main entrance, where four shed-
ding pine trees framed up the park's only landmark, a
giant billboard advertising no-questions-asked personal
loans at usury rates. An office and bank of resident mail-
boxes funneled me into a cemetery-like level of plotting
that made Fitch's trailer surprisingly difficult to find.
Every white box could be the right white box but wasn't.
An overall disdain for house numbers and porch lights
didn't help. I eventually found the correct trailer and
parked on the quiet lane fronting it.

The silence roused Rebecca from her sleep.

"We're here," I told her. "Let me go look around first."

The side entrance was carpeted with old-school ar-
tificial turf that looked like someone had pulled it up
from an abandoned mini-golf course. I took a step up
and knocked on the flimsy door. Only then did I notice
the police tape that partly sealed the gap around the
door frame.

I took out my car key and cut through the tape. One big tug on the door accomplished nothing save causing me to fall back on my ass as my hand slipped from the knob and I made the humiliating tumble off the step. The Astroturf was about as soft as the windmill hole it came from. I dusted myself off and rose to make another attempt.

"Sitting down on the job?" came a deep voice to my right.

I stared into the darkness at the back of the trailer, where a short figure stood in shadow. Every few seconds a small blip of orange flared brightly as the figure took a deep drag on what smelled like a menthol cigarette. My eyes adjusted to the night and I realized he or she was holding something long and heavy in a free hand. As I studied the shape and recalled the voice, my eyes widened.

"Julie?" I called out into the darkness and took a step toward the figure.

"I'll be anyone you want me to be, honey," came the response. "But I'll ask that you stay where you are."

The long, dark, heavy object was raised and pointed in my direction.

"There's no need for that," I said.

"That's for the person holding the shotgun to decide. Let's walk ourselves out to the street where there's some light."

I backed my way out to the lane where my car was parked under a skimpy streetlamp.

"What's the matter?" Rebecca called out, then saw

the shotgun. "Oh."

Once in the light, I got my first look at the woman holding the gun. She had a smoker's face well past the point that quitting cold turkey could reverse the effects of years of bad decisions. But smoking couldn't change her eyes. They were very soft.

"Did you hurt yourself trying to pry open that door?" she asked.

"Just my pride." I smiled.

"What do you want with Fitchie's place? You know he's dead, right?"

"Yes, I know," I told her. "I found his body."

That thankfully lowered the gun, which now was probably pointed at some unfortunate gopher a few feet underground.

"You a friend?"

I shook my head.

"Thanks for not lying. He didn't have any friends. No real ones, anyway," she reflected. "How'd you come about finding him?"

"I was looking for someone else."

She quickly picked up on the inference in my words.

"They the ones who killed him?"

The gun came up slightly. Rebecca and I shared a look.

"Someone close to me might be involved in his murder," Rebecca answered. "I'm looking for answers, too."

That kind of honesty was a curious tack while talking with someone holding a shotgun. But it seemed to work. The woman softened as she recalled her friend.

"Poor Fitchie, he wasn't the sharpest knife in the drawer. Probably didn't even know what he was getting into." She spoke of a man with a good heart, overly trusting of others who always found himself on the wrong side of a deal. "Not a lot upstairs," she reminded us. The third time she muttered a similar dig, I realized her affection for the dead man was far deeper than I had initially thought. Rebecca had made this realization long before I had.

"We sure know how to pick 'em," Rebecca mused.

"You got that right, sweetie."

"You made a comment about Fitch getting into something," I said. "You know anything about what it was?"

"He came into money, blabbering on about it being just the start. Mr. Big Shot." She laughed, but it quickly faded. "They got it all," she said, gesturing to the immensity of the night sky. "I never saw any of it."

She caught my look.

"I manage the place. Fitchie wasn't a fan of paying his bills."

"So he was behind on his rent?"

She spared me the "dim lightbulb" quip. "Pick a unit. Everyone's behind."

"Did he ever say how he came into this money?" Rebecca asked.

"He might have but I can't remember. He always had some scheme going. None out of nothing were legit." She explained that Fitch really had only two moods. He either had the world figured out (and bragged about how he did) or he whined about how that same world was out to get him. "There was no in between with him."

Or any of us, I thought.

"Where did he work?" I asked.

"He did his best work on a stool," she said, smiling. "His office is about a mile down the road. You can't miss the big red sign."

"Did he have a family?" Rebecca asked.

"He had a sister, but she's dead." After a moment she added, "Murdered."

Rebecca and I shared a look. There was something odd in the way the old woman said it.

"Why did you say it like that?" Rebecca asked.

"Because it wasn't true. I learned never to believe anything that came out of Fitchie's mouth."

"He'd make up a story about his sister being murdered?"

"You don't know Fitchie," she explained.

The woman took a deep inhalation of night air that I took as a signal that she was done reminiscing. As Rebecca and I got into the car to leave, I heard her mutter one final reflection about her friend.

"The big dummy got himself into something serious this time."

SOUTH OF SOMETHING

"What kind of beers do you have?" I asked.

The woman behind the bar did her best Helen Keller impersonation and languidly shifted her eyes from me to the tap handles right next to us. She apparently didn't have the energy or will to read them off to me. I ordered a domestic. The dirty line it traveled through, or the dirty glass it was served in, added a slightly rancid aftertaste to an otherwise unimpressive flavor profile. And being served on a chilly day in February in Bakersfield counteracted the beer's only virtue—the fact that it was cold.

SOHAR was a barfly's kind of bar. A handful of patrons worked the stools spaced far enough apart for ease of conversation and ease of detachment. There was neither great joy nor great sadness on any of their faces. They were all just content to have a warm, comfortable place in which to get systematically obliterated every night.

We listened in on the bar chatter, waiting for an opening. This crew covered a wide range of topics ranging from twin-cam fathead engines (best Harley ever produced) to zoology (lions are color-blind) to medieval history (Martin Luther had a foot fetish). The primary source of their knowledge was a mounted TV over the bar. Countless hours watching off-hour programming had given them just enough information to be truly insufferable on a wide array of topics.

I discovered a newfound empathy for the bartender. I had only been in the bar for five minutes and the blabbering was already grating on me. I'd pretend to be a deaf-mute, too, if I had to work there.

"Are you going to ask someone?" Rebecca said impatiently while pretending to sip a ginger ale.

"These sorts of things are delicate," I whispered. "I have a lot of experience in this area," continued the lecture. "Let me take the lead."

My approach was to engage someone on a harmless topic in order to establish rapport. I casually asked the gentleman next to me about the curious name of the bar—SOHAR. It worked. He took my question and launched into a detailed breakdown of famous NYC acronyms: SOHO stood for south of Houston, DUMBO—down under Manhattan Bridge overpass, TRIBECA—triangle below Canal.

"So what's the HAR stand for?" I asked.

"Huh?"

"SOHAR," I repeated. "Stands for south of what?"

"Oblivion," someone muttered several seats down.

I chuckled but no one else did.

Rebecca grew tired of my approach and tried the direct route.

"Does anyone know James Fitch?" she asked.

The room quickly got quiet.

"What you want with him?" the acronym expert asked.

I watched the man's posture on his stool. Everyone's a tough guy in front of someone who is weaker than them, and this drunk was clearly feeling his oats in front of Mr. Corporate Casual and his sick sidekick. HR had honed my skills in evaluating people, and as I studied him, I safely assumed this guy was all hot air. It was my turn to do some pushing around.

I took a long, confident gulp of my beer.

"Never mind what we want with him," I said. "Just answer the lady's fucking question."

I don't know if the welt on my head came from the actual punch or the dramatic tumble I took after it. I do know that the front of my shirt was soaked in beer from the glass I had been holding, but how the back of my shirt got wet was a mystery. I remained conscious through the entire fight—if one punch could be deemed a fight—but it was all a blurry recollection of snippets, the most embarrassing one involving an attempt to get to my feet that only succeeded in knocking over the popcorn machine. The floor becoming littered with three-day-old popcorn seemed to be the one thing that angered the patrons the most.

"You're going to have to clean that up!" the formerly

mute bartender shrieked at me.

She was joined by a chorus of murmurs, and I soon found myself with a broom in my hands. I managed to get a fraction of the popcorn into the dustpan. The rest I ground into an already sticky carpet. The bartender mercifully put an end to my cleaning duty with the exasperated words, "Just leave it."

I sheepishly returned to my stool, where I found a freshly poured glass of rancid beer, courtesy of the man who put me on my back. We spent the next five minutes trying to out-apologize each other and finally agreed that we were both at fault.

Now that we were best friends, he and everyone else unlocked the vault on James Fitch. It was almost too much information, bordering on inappropriate. Rebecca and I endured a litany of failed jobs and the long periods between them, his problems keeping tequila down, his propensity to constantly readjust himself, particularly in front of the ladies. Any attempts to provide structure to the dialogue went unheeded.

"Let's all try to stay on point," I tried, reminding them to keep their comments to the one or two important things about Fitch, at which point they provided twenty things at two levels below trivial. Several times I interjected: "That's great information…very helpful… more than we could ever use…." And yet they continued to a point where I wished we could return to the topic of color-blind lions.

But in the deluge was a handful of useful information. Arizona featured prominently in the narrative.

Fitch was raised there and still had some family outside Phoenix, they believed. A sister was mentioned several times who Fitch had repeatedly claimed had been murdered, but from the comments I heard it didn't sound like the folks in the room had believed him. I got the sense they believed a small fraction of the stuff Fitch said but didn't necessarily begrudge him for it. They all seemed to think he was a decent man.

When Rebecca questioned them on what the trailer park manager had said about Fitch coming into some money recently, the room got a little quiet.

"It wasn't much," my combatant finally said, "though Fitch kept saying 'it was only the beginning.'" It was yet another claim that no one seemed to believe, but I remembered the wad of cash Lois Hearns's ex-husband had pulled out of the freezer and wondered if they might be wrong on this one.

"Couldn't have been too much," I offered. "I saw his trailer and his landlady said he was always behind."

There were some furtive glances, very subtle, but I caught them.

"We, uh, helped him celebrate," was how someone explained where the money went. The guilt lingering after this admission was a nod to the two non-barflies in the room of a standard barfly code—one person's good fortune is everyone's good fortune.

"It's what we do," he added.

The conversation shifted to something lighter, yet no less pathetic: Fitch's love life. This topic got everyone quite excited as they recalled the long list of hags, skanks, and decent girls who all eventually figured out they were better off without Fitch. By this time I was half-listening, but then a remark recaptured my interest.

"Remember chai tea lady?" someone asked, laughing. "She was a piece of work."

"She used to bring her own organic tea bags," the bartender explained in response to my quizzical look. This all sounded familiar.

"Short, white hair? Talks like a man?"

"Not even close," the bartender replied. "Really long hair. Blond. Down to her ass."

So I was wrong about Fitch rendezvousing with Julie, but he did meet the caricaturist Lois with some regularity.

"Remember she wanted to draw my picture? Too weird," said the man on my left. "I don't get naked for nobody."

The group collectively agreed something was strange about the woman and her relationship with Fitch. Apparently they were very secretive, always talking privately in the back booth. Some believed their relationship bordered on "kinky."

"What makes you say that?" Rebecca pressed.

"There was always another guy with them."

I recalled the man in the hotel room looking for Fitch, the man who I thought had followed us in the Coupe DeVille.

"Short and bald," I filled in for them. "Looks like a big bowling ball."

"Tall and thin with a ponytail." They all laughed at me.

"You're terrible at this game!"

Maybe it wasn't the mystery man but it was someone I recognized—Lois's husband. It appeared he was much more aware of what his ex-wife was up to than he let on.

A rainy, nighttime drive over the Tejon Pass loomed larger with each glass of beer and meaningless detail about Fitch's life. But despite all attempts to extricate myself from the conversation, I couldn't make it very far from the stool. This group seemed impervious to every disengagement tactic I threw at them.

I must have checked my watch ten times but no one picked up on the cue. None of my repetitions of "Well, we should be hitting the road" seemed to work. At one point I started requesting they put their thoughts in an email—a classic corporate technique to combat people's propensity to discuss topics endlessly rather than actually work on them. Those requests went unheeded. Finally, a distraction in the form of a new customer offered us a break to run for it. They all turned to see an unfamiliar face pad into the bar. He was unfamiliar to all of them but not to Rebecca and me.

Short, bald, and stocky, the bowling ball of a man looked around the bar in the same manner he had surveyed Rebecca's hotel room. He wasn't holding a gun, but I couldn't be sure it wasn't under his coat. My theory about tough guys proved true in this instance. Everyone rightly assumed he was the toughest in the room, and in a single swoop he accomplished something I had tried to do for two-plus hours—he got them to be quiet.

I seized on that moment to slide off my stool and

quietly whispered in Rebecca's ear to follow me. We headed for the bathroom but went right past it. We scampered through the storage room and emerged in the back parking lot.

We hustled into my car and pulled around front. Standing under the SOHAR sign, the garish red light illuminating the top of his bald head, was the bowling ball man. He glared at me as I sped past his Cadillac and out onto the main drag and headed back toward Los Angeles.

The rain came sideways with such ferocity that I thought the passenger window would shatter. With each gust my car seemingly lifted up on its tires, the steering wheel becoming that much easier to turn. I fought the urge to overcompensate and jerk the car back into position, a move that had sent many a vehicle down into the gulley.

Authorities had to be near the point of closing the pass, but we continued on. We rode up on another pod of blue whales, their red taillights looming ahead. I caught Rebecca settling further into her seat, as if slightly lower in the vehicle was a safer place to be. While the wind gusts sent my sensible sedan off course a mere inch or two, they grabbed the broad sides of the trucks and rocked them back and forth.

Blue lights flashed in my mirror, and instinct led me to tap the brakes first. My heart sank at the prospect of a forced wait in traffic that could very well extend long into the night. I saw visions of a dank motel and separate beds and a sick woman far away from her next treatment. My foot pressed on the accelerator.

Glancing in the rearview mirror, I saw the comforting visual of two police cars slaloming up the hill at an ever-decreasing pace. The intended effect was a growing mass of car and truck headlights piling up behind them. The pass was officially closed, and we had made it through.

Nearing the crest, my windshield wipers stuttered over icy buildup on the glass.

"It's snowing," Rebecca whispered.

The large, wet flakes got caught up briefly in my headlights before melting into the black mass of the asphalt. My foot slowly depressed the accelerator and we gained ground on the semis. Passing the first one, I glanced over at Rebecca but got no indication that she wanted me to slow down.

The pull of wanting to be home tugged at both of us. It guided us up and over the crest and drew us down into the Valley and all the way back to Eagle Rock, where a rain-glistened sedan with two Palos Verdes detectives inside sat waiting for us with the news that Julie St. Jean was dead.

GARDENIAS

Rebecca watched the footage on one of the detec-tive's phones. To anyone passing by, it would have looked like a couple of chums killing time with mindless kitten videos. But this video was shot on a closed-circuit camera on a bridge over the Long Beach shipyard. In the early morning fog, a lone fig-ure in a black coat walked up the incline toward the bridge's broad humpback. There the figure disappeared in the mist.

"Footage from the other end doesn't have anyone coming back," the detective added.

Rebecca showed no reaction to either the video or the detective's comment. I took my cue from the two men, who respectfully looked down or turned away altogether to give her the space to absorb the news in solitude. Glancing around the room, my mind drifted to mundane thoughts of distraction—the ash in the fireplace needed to be swept out, and the place overall was due for some tidying as it had gotten unusually cluttered, with drawers open and books off the shelf.

"It could be anyone," Rebecca finally spoke.

One of the detectives sat up quickly to refute her claim but the younger one showed more maturity and secretly signaled to hold back.

"Naturally, it could be anyone," he began, but clearly didn't believe his own words. "We'll begin searching the harbor in the morning once we have daylight."

It sounded like there was more to be said.

"But?" I prodded.

"We have a strong inclination to believe it was Ms. St. Jean," he explained, even though there was no body to substantiate his statement. His partner grew impatient.

"We have visual evidence that it was her," he blurted.

After shooting his colleague a cold glare, the detective tapped his phone and presented Rebecca with a grainy photo of an older woman in a black coat. She looked straight up into the camera as if aware of its presence tucked under one of the girders.

"This was taken at the start of the bridge," he said.

"An eyewitness also confirmed he saw Ms. St. Jean walking on the bridge," his partner added.

"Who was it?" I asked, but was unprepared for the quick response.

"What do you need that information for?" the impatient detective asked. He wasn't about to let my dumb questions prolong an unwanted visit to the other side of town in the middle of the night.

"It would be helpful to know," was all I could muster for a response.

"We don't need his name," said Rebecca, saving me from further embarrassment. "It's her."

The room fell silent.

Somewhat to my surprise, Rebecca divulged a few of the details that she had previously withheld from the police, particularly the affair between Lois and Julie and the potential blackmailing scheme that arose from it. Even the impatient detective with one eye on the door settled in for this portion and took out his notebook to capture the new information. They looked pleased to finally have a narrative, made up or otherwise, that drove the facts around the murder and suicide. Working to fill in several gaps in the story, they asked questions about Julie's proclivity for violence. They were trying to determine if Lois's murder was planned or an act by a desperate person.

"She was never violent with me," Rebecca replied, an answer that divulged nothing on the surface but kept the door open for anyone wanting to believe otherwise.

As the detectives continued to probe, I watched Rebecca with an observer's distance and tried to make sense of what she was doing. Previously, she hadn't portrayed the potential blackmailing scheme as anything so dire as to warrant committing murder. According to Rebecca, Julie placed her dalliances and the complications arising from them somewhere on the level of forgetting a wedding anniversary. But the way Rebecca now conveyed it to the detectives elevated it much further on the severity scale. She wanted them to believe that Julie murdered Lois and then took her own life because of it. I followed what she was doing but couldn't figure out why.

The detectives had only five distinct questions in them but they asked twenty-five variations of each. Some would say it was deliberate in order to bring to the surface any inconsistencies in her answers. Others would say it was simply out of incompetence. Either way a ten-minute interview took two hours. Rebecca was a willing participant, but I wasn't. My eyes grew heavier with each repeated question-and-answer until I finally succumbed and fell asleep.

"We'll be in touch, ma'am," said a voice, rousing me from my nap. I rose with them and walked the detectives to the door. There were more pleasantries as the cold night air brought some clarity back to my head. The young detective was almost halfway down the walk when I called him back.

"Detective," I said, then lowered my voice. "You're going to search for the body tomorrow?"

"As soon as there's daylight," he replied, but picked up on the unstated question and continued. "There's a lot of ship traffic under that bridge," he intoned. That simple statement spared me the grim details of what likely happened to the body but also told me that the likelihood of finding it was slim to none. "I'm sorry," he added.

Rebecca was already heading to bed by the time I went back in the house.

"You were pretty chatty," I scolded.

"They're looking for answers, just like us."

"You gave them misleading ones."

"You went along with it."

"While I was awake."

"We both know Julie's not dead."

I certainly had my doubts. These were borne mainly out of the events relayed to us by the detectives but also out of what I knew about Julie. Over the years, I'd seen her backed into a corner when it looked like our firm was finally going to move in a new direction with employee engagement. She never panicked. She quietly and confidently prepared for a fight that she always won.

I grew to fear her at those times.

"It's unlikely they'll find her body," I said.

"More than unlikely," Rebecca corrected. "She was here tonight."

"How do you know?"

Rebecca gave a wistful half-smile.

"I can still smell her perfume."

Julie's lingering presence lifted Rebecca's spirits, but it lowered mine. The hope of a simple resolution grew dimmer with each development. If Rebecca was right, Julie had staged her suicide—which meant she never wanted to be found. And now there was a new wrinkle: As I studied the untidiness of the room, I realized that Julie had been looking for something.

What that was I didn't know.

A BREAK FROM THE MUNDANE

Fifteen seconds into the phone call to Phoenix, it was readily apparent that Detective Richard Fortin had a personality fitting for the common nickname of his given one.

"Who?" He made me repeat my name for the third time, at which point he added, "Never heard of you."

"I know, sir," I explained, "we've never met before."

"Then why are you calling me?"

He overlooked the fact that technically he had called me, or in any case had returned the message I'd left on his answering machine.

"What's this about again?" he peppered.

The retired detective interrupted my attempts to explain why I was reaching out to him with more questions, which he rattled off with barely any time in between for replies. As I struggled to get a word in, I got the sense that he found this act quite entertaining. I conjured up the image of an old man, some seventeen years off the force, utterly bored with retirement and oddly grateful to have this little one-sided sparring session with a stranger on the phone. Perhaps it reminded him of the good old days, when he could talk over anyone he damn well pleased in an interrogation room. I didn't want to begrudge him a respite from the drudgery of retirement, but I also didn't want to be a pushover and be bullied.

"Hello?" he asked into the phone after I stopped responding. "You still there?"

I smiled to myself for having read him correctly and because of how quickly his tune changed. There was a little fear in his voice that this pest on the phone might buzz off and actually leave him alone.

I let that fear hang in the air for a few seconds longer.

"I'm here," I replied.

"Oh, I thought you'd hung up."

I gave him a little more silence just so he didn't think he could launch into another one of his bullying rants.

"What do you need from me, Mr. Restic?" he finally asked, sounding compliant enough to remember my name and in a tone that felt genuine. It was time to get straight to the purpose of my call. I dropped a few names Badger had supplied me with; this seemed to work because the detective immediately relaxed on the phone. I then asked about Margaret Fitch.

"Maggie?" he confirmed. "She was a part-time prostitute and a full-time drug addict. Lost her teeth at twenty-five and what little beauty she had long before that." It sounded all too similar to her loser brother in Bakersfield. "She was one of our regulars. I knew her before I made detective. Every time you pick them up," he reminisced, "you give them the same old song-and-dance about cleaning up, getting back on track. She wasn't a bad girl inside. You warn them that they have to change their ways or else. Else what?" he asked rhetorically, perhaps even recalling the response he got from Maggie every time he uttered the warning at two in the morning. "You think there's no way the human body can keep taking that kind of abuse, that it's only a matter of time before we find them dead somewhere, but goddamn if they don't just keep showing up year after year!"

The detective gave a half-wheeze, half-laugh. It took him a moment to collect himself.

"We crossed paths again years later when I made detective," he remembered. "I was working narcotics. Picked her up on a felony possession charge." Detective Fortin recalled the arrest with remarkable accuracy. I knew this because I had a copy of the arrest report in front of me, courtesy of Badger. How he secured this sort of documentation was a question I left unasked. It seemed the prudent path.

"Enough for intent to distribute," he continued. "This was back in the War on Drugs days when it wasn't a good time to be getting caught." Detective Fortin reflected on a detail that had piqued my interest when reading the report. "I'll admit, the size of the score was a little strange for Maggie, but you sort of learn never to question what an addict can do. For all I know she stole it from someone."

The old detective finally grew tired of answering so many questions and thought he'd reverse roles for a minute or two.

"Why the interest in Maggie after all these years?"

I explained how her brother Jimmy had recently been murdered in Sierra Madre, likely because of his connection to a blackmailing scheme.

"Never earned an honest dollar in his life," the detective commented.

"Did you know him well?" I asked.

"Not really. He was a punk kid who grew up into a punk adult and then left Phoenix. You say he lived in Bakersfield?"

"Yes."

"Their loss, our gain" was his summation of Fitch's impact on the world.

"His friends said he came into some money recently."

"He had friends?"

I explained that Fitch talked a big game about coming into a hefty amount of money. Some of his friends believed him, most didn't. But they all heard how bitter he was—there should have been more. "People seem to think he got it from his sister."

There was a long pause. It was now my turn to check in on the voice at the other end.

"I'm here," the detective answered.

I allowed myself to get excited as this development had gotten the wheels spinning in the old cop's head.

I queued up several questions about the Fitch siblings and then several more that would probe their relationship with Julie St. Jean. Perhaps this was the thread I had been searching for that linked all these seemingly disparate characters.

"What do you think of that claim?" I asked.

"Sounds like the rants of a good-for-nothing who's convinced himself the world's at fault for all of his failures." After a short pause, he added sadly, "Sorry, didn't mean to be so coldhearted. I've just heard that pitch too many times."

"So there's no chance Maggie came into some money?" I asked.

"Let's put it this way," the detective answered with conviction, "if Maggie had any money there was only one place it went."

"I see," I responded, as only a non-addict can in areas they know nothing about. I had one more question but it was more out of an impulse for tidying up than any real need for information. "What about the claim that his sister was murdered?"

"Could have been."

"But?"

"But we'll never know. She never appeared for her court date."

"What happened to her?"

Detective Fortin said she was held in custody for a few days and eventually was let out on bail. No one ever saw her again. He figured she was dead.

"I always felt like there was something more to that

case," he said, but then quickly doused whatever spark flared deep down in his investigative soul. "Was she murdered?" he asked for me. "Who knows."

Out of respect for the deceased, he left off the last part:

"Who cares?"

Our phone call was coming to an end, although it had really ended long before the official conclusion. When I'd gotten Detective Fortin's name from Badger, I'd hoped the past in Arizona would provide the details I needed to make sense of what was happening today in Los Angeles.

"Does the name Julie St. Jean mean anything to you?"

"Who?" he answered, snuffing out what little hope of a connection I had left.

I should have hung up fifteen minutes earlier but felt oddly guilty at denying the old detective a break from his day to reminisce about a time when his life was a little more eventful. I lit the spark but then had to extinguish it.

"I don't want to take up more of your time," I told him as a way to disengage, but then wished I had chosen different words because I knew the response that was coming.

"Hell, I got nothing but time."

A SHARED DISLIKE

I spent the afternoon in yet another review of the dismal employee engagement survey. It was as if management couldn't accept the results and thought further review of them would somehow change the numbers. For this round they included some of the actual people quoted in the survey. The parade of low-level associates misinterpreted the invitation as a legitimate call for their opinions.

One young woman was particularly passionate while explaining how the organization didn't take her development seriously. She described how important it was to marry her personal development—"two-thirds of the way back to my pre-baby weight"—with her professional one. The poor thing's voice cracked and her neck grew splotchy as she expressed how "abandoned" she felt. There was a lot of head-nodding in the room but disappointment was clear on the faces of the committee members. They weren't getting what they wanted: a convenient justification on which they could pin the low scores.

After work, I decided to waste an extra fifteen minutes in standstill traffic with a detour to Burbank. I had placed several calls to Hearns and never heard back, so I hoped to catch him in his garage. The stash of money in his freezer and the rendezvous with Fitch in Bakersfield told me he wasn't exactly being truthful and I needed to figure out why.

The city had been granted a one-day respite from the El Niño rains, and for the first time in a long while the stars and moon shone in the night sky. I gave myself an hour and spent nearly all of it waiting outside the house. The few headlights that came down the street were either residents or folks zigzagging their way across the Valley to avoid the freeway. But one set of lights caught my attention. It appeared at the end of the street and slowed as it neared the house. Unless Lois's ex-husband had traded in his pickup for a trendy, electric-cell vehicle, I was out of luck. The car purred to a near-silent crawl as it glided by where I was parked on the opposite side of the road. The driver had his head turned toward the house, so I couldn't get a good look, but the Hearns house was clearly of great interest to him.

I watched the taillights gain some distance as the car continued down the street, but then the brake lights went on as the driver slowed and turned the vehicle around to head back toward me. I ducked to get out of the glare of the oncoming headlights, but it turned out I didn't need to because the driver switched them off long before arriving at the house. The vehicle nestled into an empty spot some thirty yards down the road and sat there for a few minutes.

I didn't have to get out to investigate because I was pretty certain I knew who was behind the wheel. My suspicion was confirmed some ten minutes later when the person got out and skulked in the dark under the ficus canopy. A slim shaft of moonlight briefly illuminated his face.

Bronson Thibideux headed for the garage and then the walkway leading up to the front door. But then he surprised me and instead turned to the side of the house and disappeared into the darkness behind it.

I watched the front windows of the house but saw no sign of any movement inside. After ten minutes of waiting in the car, to the point where the condensation obscured most of my view, I got out to investigate.

I worked my way around the side of the house opposite from the way Bronson had gone, but kept as close to the structure as possible. It wasn't exactly a burglar's delight the way the moon lit up the yard. I stayed in the overhang's shadow and passed three closed windows before coming to one left ajar. Half of the curtain hung outside and was darkening on the damp sill. Through the slat I watched a faint penlight dance around the room.

Bronson moved from one of the back bedrooms to the next one, which served as a mini-office. I followed along outside the house. From the corner of the window

I watched him alight on the accordion file folder that Hearns used to store all of his documents. Bronson riffled through the various compartments until his fingers stopped their dancing and pulled out a thick document, which he studied in the light. He apparently had found what he came for because he shoved the document inside his coat and made his way back through the house and straight out the main door.

I waited five minutes before returning to my car because I wanted to make sure he was gone. Looping around the garage, I passed by the same window where I'd spied Hearns shove a large sheaf of bills into his pants pocket. The door to the freezer where the money was stored caught the moon's steely half-light and glowed like a white beacon. I paused. It only caught the moonlight because it had been left open. I peered into the window and caught something else out of place in the immaculate garage.

Something large and shapeless lay crumpled on the cement floor. I couldn't see the ponytail but I knew who it was.

I ran toward the front of the garage and tugged at the rolling door. It rattled open. I searched for the string serving as a light switch. A fluorescent light flickered on and revealed a grim sight.

Hearns had clearly been worked over. His arm was bent at an unnatural angle and looked broken. I was certain he was dead, but the garish light seemed to jolt him out of his stupor. His eyes fluttered open and he attempted to move his broken arm to cover them but then thought otherwise.

I quickly dialed 911 and gave them the relevant information.

Hearns didn't seem to to recognize me. If anything, he looked a little fearful.

"It's okay," I told him, after hanging up the phone. "You remember me, right?"

He looked far worse awake than when I'd feared him dead.

"Remember we talked the other day?" I coaxed.

He shut his eyes and parted his lips at the same time, but had only enough energy for one movement. His teeth were covered in a pink gouache and a deeper red at the gum line where the blood was thicker.

"Dirty cops," he groaned.

"That's right." I smiled, recalling our mutual hatred for all things law enforcement. "Dirty cops. Who did this to you?"

Despite my repeatedly asking him for a name, he said nothing more. He apparently had enough energy for just those two words. His chest swelled with long, slow breaths. I heard sirens in the distance and knew I had to act.

"Hang in there," I told him and ran back around into the house. I rushed to the room where Bronson had left the accordion file and thumbed through the slots. The sirens grew steadily louder. I needed to hurry up.

I ran through phone bills, electric bills, cable bills, and then finally came upon bank statements. The sirens were deafening, which meant they were on the street.

There wasn't enough time to run back to my car, so I grabbed a handful of the most recent statements and stuffed them into my sock. I ran back to the front door and closed it behind me just as the first police cruiser pulled up.

The officer who appeared first was justifiably suspicious and focused all his attention on me, barely acknowledging that a man was in critical condition on the floor of a garage a few feet away. The officer pointed out the victim to the arriving paramedics but continued to pepper me with questions.

I made up a story about dropping in on Hearns to deliver my condolences for the death of his wife, but kept getting distracted by the weight in the sock under my pant leg. The bank statements were slipping. I manically adjusted my stance to keep them from falling out. It didn't go unnoticed.

"You all right?" he asked.

"What? Yeah, I'm fine. It was just such a surprise seeing him like that," I said, trying to deflect.

"No, you're moving around a lot," he said. "You been drinking?"

"Me?"

He waited for my response.

"No, I worked today. I haven't been drinking."

It didn't look like he believed me. I needed to get his attention off of me.

"You know," I started, "there was one thing that seemed a bit off. Probably nothing but you never know."

He waited impatiently for me to tell him.

"There was a suspicious-looking man here when I drove up."

"Is that right?"

"Yeah, he was in one of those fancy electric cars. Kind of hanging around the house when I got here. Didn't think anything of it at the time but I took down his license plate if you want it...."

THE WEIGHT OF WISDOM

I made the trek up to Pat Faber's floor and swung by the break room for my morning coffee, planning to hang out there until I "bumped" into him coming in for the day. These casual encounters were the key to managing my personal brand, and since I was awake at this ungodly hour I might as well get credit for it.

Rebecca and I had spent the night processing the latest developments. Arizona and Fitch's "murdered" sister were dead ends, but Lois and the blackmail scheme were alive and well. What we couldn't figure out was over what. Sitting in front of the fire, I stared into the flames as if the answer lay somewhere in the hot coals. And when it didn't appear, I added more logs until we both had to push our chairs back from the excessive heat emanating from the hearth.

"That's it for me," Rebecca whispered. She got up and padded off to bed. "You're not going to figure it out tonight," she admonished. "Get some rest yourself."

I didn't heed her advice and spent the next couple of hours staring blankly into the fire, thinking about the woman down the hall. We had never openly acknowledged Rebecca staying at my place as a longer-term solution, but it was becoming just that. It was simply easier to have her nearby as we worked on unraveling the mess of Julie's disappearance. The other reason never openly addressed was that I truthfully didn't want her stay to end.

I was afraid that once Rebecca returned to her life—either in the downtown hotel or across the city in Palos Verdes—our relationship would return to its previous state: that of two people who spent many hours together at work but for all intents and purposes were strangers. Rebecca and I had gotten into a nice routine around her treatments and the difficult hours after they were over. She never verbalized it, but I could tell how much she appreciated what I was doing for her. And I never told her just how good it felt to be needed. The fear underlying all of it, however, was a growing recognition that I couldn't help with either of her problems.

"First cup?" a smiling Pat Faber said to me, as I filled one of the communal mugs with coffee.

With a stiff neck from having fallen asleep in the rocking chair, I had to turn my entire body to address him. But before I could answer, Pat surveyed the scene and answered his own question for me with a disappointed nod.

"I just finished my breakfast," he felt the need to

add, and put his dirty bowl in the sink for someone else to load in the dishwasher. To Pat, work was about proving you did more than others. The fact that he had already had multiple cups of coffee and a bowl of instant oatmeal before my first mug confirmed his position as chief rock-buster on the chain gang.

"I usually skip breakfast," I countered pathetically. "So many meetings I often forget to eat!"

It was a poor attempt at waving the "busy" moniker. Pat barely acknowledged it.

"Where are we with P of O?"

I knew he was referring to Julie's outfit but I pretended to have to think about it for a moment. His unnecessary use of the acronym was a signal of strength that I needed to challenge by downplaying its significance.

"P of O..." I repeated, waiting for him to spell it out for me.

He didn't oblige. The awkward silence started to reflect poorly on me, so I had to fill it.

"Power of One!" I finally caught it. "Thought you were referring to one of the other really big initiatives we got going on," I proffered as an excuse. "Yup, all good with them. Moving along, meeting the milestones, tracking well on the deliverables timeline...."

Pat didn't have to say anything—I could hear the skepticism in his silent glare.

I very quickly began to regret coming in early because I was wholly unprepared for a discussion with Pat on this topic. The last time we'd spoken I'd let him think we were moving forward with Power of One, knowing full well that I would get them to quit long before they ever ruined me with another display of inanity. But here I was in a position in which I had to actually defend them. The perversity of the corporate world was on full display—my survival was tied to making another man's idea a success, and the person hammering me was the very buffoon who had the idea in the first place.

I allowed all my frustrations to take over the moment. I was annoyed at being outplayed by this fool and at the growing reality that I couldn't help a woman who really needed it. And those frustrations manifested themselves in my making bold statements that I knew I couldn't deliver.

"Hey, P-a-t," I began, overly enunciating every letter in his name. I can't be sure but I believe I even jammed a two-fingered point into his bony chest. "Make no mistake. You—will be—blown A-W-A-Y."

"I love the passion," he commended. "Make sure you deliver."

I spent the next two hours shaking my head in disgust while staring at a blank screen in the quiet of my office. My assistant checked up on me after I skipped two straight meetings.

"Are you not feeling well?" she asked. "I heard you moaning."

Her voice brought me out of a stupor.

"I'll be fine," I told her, but didn't really believe it. There was so little to be sanguine about when assessing the various outcomes to the entire affair. Julie was either dead or a crook or both. Without Julie, there was no consultant business. That left Rebecca on her own, sick, and woefully in debt, and it left me having to justify my highly visible promotion of such a claptrap outfit.

"I'll be fine," I repeated, but this time I had to believe it.

There was no other choice. The last thing Rebecca needed was a full severance of her only revenue stream. I decided I needed to save the contract for her. And to do that, I needed to actually deliver on the impossible— I needed to present Julie's nonsense and make it zing.

"Please cancel the rest of my meetings today," I told my assistant. "There's something I need to work on."

I went down into the bowels of the building to get the Power of One binders out of the trunk of my car. Hefting the first box out nearly pulled my feet out of my shoes. I decided not to risk a back injury and lightened the load. Taking out the first few rows of binders from the box revealed why it was so heavy.

The bottom was lined with neatly stacked packs of hundred-dollar bills. The blue lettering that banded the packs screamed in the trunk light that each was worth ten grand.

"Two-point-six million," I said.

Rebecca stared wistfully at the stacks of money. Badger grunted somewhere deep in his throat and then for some inexplicable reason felt the need to cup his balls in his palm. He caught our glances and quickly removed his hand.

"Are you sure you're okay keeping the money here?"

Rebecca asked him.

Badger nodded solemnly.

"You think it will be safe?" I asked, already beginning to doubt the decision to bring the money to Badger's. The back room of his office in Echo Park also served as his residence. It was a depressing space with no natural light and a mustiness that caught me in the back of the throat. I saw his suit hanging on a pipe next to a make-shift shower and understood the ever-present smell of mold whenever he wore it.

"It is in my care," he said, and bowed like some an-cient warrior. "No harm will come to it."

"All this old-speak is actually making me more ner-vous than anything," I told him.

"Don't worry," he reassured me, "no one is breaking in here."

Unless there was a rash of refried-bean-can robber-ies in the neighborhood, I didn't see why anyone would. That was partly the reason for selecting Badger's "home" as the place to hide the money. No one would think to look for it here. Also, despite my misgivings about his lustful interest in the money, he was the only person I really trusted.

I figured the money had to have been placed in the box by Julie, but there was a minute when I doubted even that. Although Rebecca and I had achieved a level of familiarity, there was still a distance between us that I felt I might never close. But, I reasoned, if Rebecca had known about the money, she certainly wouldn't have let me drive all over town with it in the back of my trunk. And after the discussion we'd had about finances, I can't imagine her tone would have been as dire if she had a spare couple of million in cash lying around.

"Could this be from the sale of your company?" Badger asked, which was greeted with a quick laugh from Rebecca.

Rebecca explained that Power of One's intellectual property might be worth a little, the name itself a little more. But the only real "value" in the company was Julie herself.

Once again I marveled at how nothingness could be worth so much.

"The money had to come from somewhere," I said. "Could Julie have been skimming?"

"Julie did all of her reckless spending in plain sight," Rebecca replied. "There was no concealing that part of her life."

I began to wonder if Julie was involved in something that plumbed a lot deeper than I first suspected. Lois's murder and the secret stash of cash in her ex-husband's freezer, the Bakersfield rendezvous with Fitch, the long-forgotten tragedy of an addict sibling who disappeared from sight after her arrest, and the sudden reappearance of the bowling ball man all pointed to something that happened three decades in the past, one state over.

"It has to be Fitch's sister," Badger surmised. "Some connection to that dope arrest."

Rebecca and I bandied a few jokes about Julie as a

drug kingpin. Of the three, we were the only two who found it amusing.

"Badger's got a feeling about this one," he intoned.

"Badger doesn't know what he's talking about," I mocked. "I agree there's some connection—but Julie St. Jean dealing drugs? You forget she was living a quiet librarian's life in Sierra Madre in the early 1980s. You really think she's running drugs on the side?"

"Listen, hondo," he shot back, "explain why a junkie is holding that much product."

Badger referenced a detail that I remembered from my discussion with Detective Fortin. The felony charge indicated an intent to distribute a very large amount of drugs.

"It couldn't have belonged to the sister," Badger explained. "It had to be someone else's. Also, think about it a minute. How does someone like Maggie Fitch, who was living under an overpass at the time of her arrest, come up with the money to post bond on a felony drug charge? Only rich people can play that game."

Rebecca shot me a look. He was winning her over. And if I was being honest, the same was happening with me.

"And after all these years Fitch finally decides it's time to declare his sister legally dead?" Badger continued. "At the same time that he gets wrapped up in this affair? Don't tell me they aren't connected."

Something then caught my eye that confirmed Badger's theory.

I grabbed a stack of bills and thumbed through them. I did the same for the next stack and then a few more just to be sure. They all had the old design with the small portrait of Ben Franklin. And every bill belonged to a series no later than 1984.

"Old money," Badger said with a smile.

ROOMMATES

Despite Rebecca's assertion that she and Julie never delved much into each other's past, she made an exception on this because it might have been the only path that would lead us to her wife. There were gaps in the narrative Badger provided about the young woman from Vero Beach, Florida, who had become a librarian in Sierra Madre and then an executive coach and consultant guru living in a glass palace in Palos Verdes. Viewing her life as a résumé, those were not very credible transitions between roles. The narrative wasn't "tracking," as recruiters liked to say, and begged further exploration. The bag full of hundred-dollar bills printed before 1985 helped me prioritize at which point in time to start.

As I drove north into the canyons, I watched the rain clouds hung up in the mountains ahead of us and wondered if the long climb into Sierra Madre would

put us square in their midst. My windshield was peppered with a slight drizzle, not enough to warrant the
wipers but enough to make it difficult to see too far
ahead. Driveways along the left side of the street were
buttressed with pale sandbags two or three rows high.
Mini-sandbars left by last night's run-off added further
protection, or perhaps served as perfect ramps to breach
the fortifications during the next deluge.

We headed west at the downtown intersection and
found the Sierra Madre Library after a few long blocks.
It was a low structure of reddish brick and pitched
roofs that read proudly from the 1950 civic-building
handbook.

"Can you see Julie as a librarian?" I asked as we
made our way inside.

"To be honest, I've never seen her read a book,"
she replied.

"No one reads anymore."

I braced for the pungent smell of ten-day-old body
odor and stale urine and instead was greeted with an
inviting, almost homey scent. My only interaction with
libraries these days was when I used the one in downtown LA as a shortcut on my way to a favorite lunch
spot on Flower Street. The Central Library hadn't yet
officially been declared a new chapter of Midnight Mis-
sion, but its denizens treated it as one, particularly during the rainy season.

Another surprise but a less welcome one was the age
of the women behind the desk. I had hoped for elderly
spinsters but instead saw several young women who ob-

viously hadn't been here when Julie manned the card catalogue. After a quick discussion with the woman at the front desk, we were guided to a back room where the town's volunteer archivist donated precious hours to sit and do nothing at the library when she could be doing the very same thing at home.

"The bathroom is back by the entrance," she said, mistakenly thinking that whoever came upon this room would do so only by accident. I had to explain that we weren't lost patrons but that we were actually interested in learning more about some of the town's residents. "You've come to the right place," she said. "Born and raised in Sierra Madre, my great—"

"Julie St. Jean," I jumped in before she ran through her entire ancestry.

The old woman studied me.

"You're the man who found the body," she stated.

"Yes, how do you know that?"

"Oh," she said, a blush rising on her cheeks, "I heard there was a commotion up that way and thought I'd drop in and see what the to-do was about."

I secretly added Town Busybody to her growing list of qualifications. This was a good development because these sorts of people know everything in a small town, particularly the shadowy parts of people's lives.

"The police say they don't have any credible leads," she said in a way that begged for me to confirm or deny that statement. I let it hang there unanswered. "Are you family?" the old woman finally asked.

"Yes," I jumped in before Rebecca could reply.

It felt like a feeler question and I wanted to see where it would lead.

"Surprised to hear that. Miss St. Jean never had any close family...understandably," she added, with a curious look in Rebecca's direction. "Listen," she began, in a manner that signaled something juicy, "we're a small town with small-town values but we don't judge. She was a gentle soul, kept to herself, quiet as a church mouse. She could have been more open about it but that wasn't Julie."

None of it sounded remotely like the Julie I knew, the woman most comfortable with a spotlight permanently affixed on her.

There was something peculiar about the way the archivist described Julie. She used that persistently positive tone reserved for retirement parties and eulogies and someone who, when trying to sum up a career or life, can muster only a white-washed meandering devoid of anything remotely unique. My suspicion was confirmed with her next question.

"When did she pass?"

"Excuse me?" I asked. Unless she trolled the newspapers for local crime logs, there was no way for her to have heard of the supposed suicide.

"Isn't that why you're here? To claim her money?"

Out of the corner of my eye, I caught Rebecca shooting me a look.

"What money?" I asked unconvincingly.

"What money," she admonished. "Like I told you, we don't judge around here." It certainly felt like she was doing just that. "The Social Security can't be much," she mused, "but that house is certainly worth a pretty penny. And you want to know if anyone else might have a claim on it."

"And if that was the case?" I asked.

The old woman leaned in.

"If I were you, I'd be concerned about that 'roommate' of hers. Who knows with those crackpots up in Sacramento, giving away the state as they are to the illegals. Look at what they've done to the sanctity of marriage. Who knows who gets what with the laws now."

We had a growing sense that the Julie and Lois affair was much more than a recent thing, perhaps even predating the long-term one Julie had with Rebecca. The specter of a double life followed us out of the library and along the silent drive over to the coffee shop, where we hoped to find more answers.

"You just getting out now?" The old man smirked as he poured me a cup of coffee. Rebecca waved him off as she sat down at the counter.

"Just a little misunderstanding," I explained. "You know, you didn't have to call the cops," I told him when he finished pouring.

"I'll decide what I can and can't do," he responded. "But in this case, I never called them."

One detail that supported his assertion—something that had been gnawing at me since I spent the afternoon at the police station—was the speed in which the police had arrived on the scene. Rebecca and I were at the house for at most three minutes, and yet they were there en masse right after I entered the lower level. I sympathized with the plight of a small-town cop with nothing to do but that was a surprising response time, particularly when you consider the circuitous route it took to get up to the house itself. This all led me to believe that someone tipped them off long before our arrival. The officers were waiting there the entire time.

The coffee shop was quiet this late in the afternoon. A few patrons nursed mugs of black coffee and stared out the windows. It was colder than during our last visit and the rain was really picking up. The old man caught Rebecca glancing at the woodstove and quietly came out from behind the counter to add another log.

"How's the neighborhood dealing with the murder?" I asked.

"That's a dumb question."

"Is it?"

"Yes, it is."

He was right, but I still had to defend it to save face.

"I figure you don't get much of that kind of action up this way."

He humored me with a long, silent stare.

"What can I get you?"

"We're looking for a little more information on Julie St. Jean's roommate," I told him.

"Can't help you there."

"Do you know her?"

"I know of her. She isn't a regular."

"What do you think of her?" I probed.

"I just told you I barely know her."

"Have you seen her around lately?"

"I quit the neighborhood watch group years ago. What's with all the questions?" he asked with one of his own.

"Julie St. Jean's wanted for questioning in her murder."

The flip responses ceased. He looked at me, glanced in Rebecca's direction, then settled back on me.

"When's the last time you saw her?" I asked.

"Who?"

"Julie."

"Long time."

"*Long* can mean a lot of different things."

"Decades," he amended. "Ever since she moved to Florida."

Julie's rendezvous with Lois at the home up the street were frequent enough that someone must have run into her over all these years. The old man had to have seen her or at a minimum heard about it from the gossipmongers within this tight-knit community. Either way, he wasn't being truthful.

"You mentioned Florida," I said. "You said something similar when we were first here."

"Did I?" he deflected.

"The helpful woman at the library said the same thing."

"Well then, now you know it's a fact," he said dismissively.

"Julie never moved to Florida. She never left Los Angeles. She may have moved out of the house up the road some time back but she hasn't actually stayed away. She's been using it for…other purposes."

The old man wanted to interject, most likely with another dismissive comment, but I wouldn't let him. The look on his face foreshadowed two possibilities— finally bending or getting so annoyed he would kick us out. I continued to push.

"I think you knew all this already but for some reason you don't want to acknowledge it. Everyone and their sister knows what's going on up the road but it's some big mystery to you. And you can smile and throw out every flippant response in the book but just be clear that every time you do, you're only convincing me that you know more about Julie than anyone in this town."

The few patrons in the room stopped their conversations and, with ears bent toward the counter, waited for the old man's response.

"Why can't you just leave that poor woman alone?"

"I'm her wife," Rebecca stated.

I watched him take a deep breath, like someone about to agree to something they don't want to do. The old man didn't like the cut of my jib but he clearly had some concern for Rebecca.

"I don't know much," he said softly. Although he addressed me, it was clear he was talking to Rebecca.

"Were you close?" she asked.

"Julie was one of our regulars," he started. "Never a counter patron, though. Nope, never the counter. It was too far away from the stove."

"She always complains about being cold," said Rebecca.

"That sounds right," the old man recalled. "Probably the real reason she moved back to Florida."

"Why do you keep saying that?" Rebecca asked gently. "Don't feel you have to hold back because of me. I'm fully aware of everything that's going on."

"How long have you been married, hon?" he asked.

"Officially, seven years. Together for three times that."

"I always liked Julie," he stated. Unlike the pleasantries we'd heard from the archivist, the old man's words felt genuine. "But I'm being truthful when I say I haven't seen her in a long time."

"With all due respect," I cut in, "she's been at the house up the road pretty regularly for many years. You have to know what's been going on."

"Don't lecture me, son. I know what's going on up the road."

"You know about what the house is used for?"

"Everyone does."

Rebecca and I shared a look.

"Then how can you say you haven't seen Julie in decades?"

"Because she hasn't been here," he answered. "Can't you get that through your thick skull?"

The old man was past the point of losing his patience and was fast approaching the point of shutting down entirely. Rebecca sensed it, too.

"I believe you," she said. "But please, just humor me." She then used her phone to pull up a picture of herself and Julie standing before an ocean vista. "The woman on the left."

The man leaned back to get a better look at the photo.

"That's not Julie," the man said.

"Who is it?"

"That's her old roommate."

DRY ERASE

When did Julie leave for Florida?" asked Badger.

"Summer of 1986," I recalled, and simultaneously wrote the date and event down on the whiteboard in my office.

"That's right around the time Fitch's sister disappeared."

I wrote that down, too, but in a different color.

I captured everything we had discovered on the board to create one big timeline stretching from today all the way back to the early 1980s. I drew solid lines between connected events and dotted lines where I had a hunch there was a connection but couldn't confirm it. I'd always felt as though a thread tied these random periods together but only now that I could visually represent them on the board did they take on meaning.

Badger didn't share my enthusiasm.

"Why do you keep writing down everything I say?"

he asked innocently.

I was momentarily flummoxed. Whiteboarding was the darling of the corporate world and the truest signal to everyone watching that there was some serious strategizing going on. While the guy in front of the old-fashioned flip chart was a mere "note taker," the one in front of a whiteboard was an "ideator." I'd mastered whiteboarding sessions years ago, much to the benefit of my career advancement, and in all that time no one had ever questioned such a proven approach before.

"I'm trying to visualize a complex scenario by putting words to paper," I explained, even though there was no paper involved. And for a guy who never used paper, this was clearly a foreign concept to Badger. "Breaking it up into snackable bites allows us to overcome the enemy of all strategic problem-solving—inertia. As we've done here, capturing the seemingly random events from the past paints a clearer picture from which we can deliver viable solution sets."

Badger nodded.

"What are you going to do with it when you're done?"

"It's the process that has value, not the output."

"So you won't actually do anything with this?"

"I mean, I might take a photo of it with my phone."

He nodded again.

"And do what with it?"

"Just to have in case we need to reference it...or something."

As he was about to ask his next undermining question, I quickly grabbed the eraser and wiped the board clean.

"Let's get back on track," I huffed, and sat down at my desk. "So where were we?"

We returned to the topic that had everyone's head spinning—that the Julie St. Jean we all knew was actually Maggie Fitch from Arizona. I had assumed that all of the "roommate" talk in Sierra Madre referred to the affair between Julie and Lois. But it now looked like it was in regard to an entirely different affair, one that transpired some thirty years earlier.

Badger riffed on how it might have played out.

"Say Maggie jumps bail," he started. "First thing, she needs to get out of town fast. I could see picking Los Angeles. Her brother was out here by then and she probably ran to family."

According to the old man at the coffee shop, Maggie began renting a room at Julie's house in Sierra Madre shortly after her arrest in Phoenix. Maybe it started as a business relationship but it apparently turned into something more. The town gossip at the library said as much.

"Within a few years, Julie has quit her long-term job at the library and up and moves everything across the country," I added to his narrative.

"She doesn't take everything," Badger corrected. "The house was never sold."

The old man at the coffee shop made this point. Maggie continued to live at the house for some period. This raised a few eyebrows over coffee in the shop but nothing more than that. Julie had always been a private woman and neighbors felt it better to leave well enough alone. After a few months Maggie moved out and apparently took Julie's identity with her. This explained the age discrepancy on "Julie's" original W-9.

I sat back and smiled. The fact that the ageless guru wasn't so youthful made me feel better about my own losing battle with time. I also admittedly enjoyed knowing that the sage of the corporate world was actually a former drug addict who had sold her body for the next score. But what really warmed my heart was thinking about how Pat Faber had made critical life decisions based on this woman's advice. I temporarily basked in a pool of *Schadenfreude*, but then I remembered watching Rebecca as she processed the same information the night before.

We had driven home in silence from the coffee shop in a rain so heavy it felt like we hydroplaned all the way back to Eagle Rock. I built a fire and warmed some soup, the only thing Rebecca could still stomach anymore. She was wasting away in front of me; the already rail-thin woman somehow had gotten thinner over the last week. The untouched bowl sat in her lap as she stared silently into the fire. After what seemed like twenty minutes, she finally whispered:

"She's the same person."

"You think Julie and Maggie are one and the same," I said.

"So do you," Rebecca replied, "and that's not what I meant." The two who had never delved into each other's past now had to come to some sort of reconciliation with it. Rebecca's was one of reluctant acceptance. This new information about Julie's real identity didn't change the person she was in love with. After a moment's reflection, she added, "She's the same person to me."

Badger continued to build the narrative.

"Maggie reinvents herself in Los Angeles. She needs a new identity, a new everything."

"So she takes on Julie's identity and starts fresh in the leadership coaching business."

"Let's hope that's all she took," Badger shot back.

He verbalized the unstated fear behind all of the arched eyebrows, the whispers in the coffee shop, the back-of-the-library conversations—that the real Julie never made that trip to Florida after all.

"I'll check that county in Florida where she was raised. If she went back there, there must be some record of it." And not that I needed further clarification, but Badger added, "I'll start with the death records."

"How does the money work?" I asked. "We know it's old so it probably originates from Maggie's time in Arizona and is connected to her arrest."

"It could have been the real Julie's money."

"That doesn't match the librarian profile."

"It has to be drug money, then."

"That sits for thirty years," I added. "Why didn't she spend it?"

"How do you know she didn't?"

I had heard the story of Power of One's rise from obscurity countless times over the years. Self-made people have an insatiable appetite for chronicling the steps leading to their success, and Julie was no exception. In all of the retellings, I never got a sense that there was a large pool of money funding the business.

"Also, the money only surfaced in the last year or two," I added. "Large transfers to Lois, payments to Fitch, activity at a secret bank account in Pasadena."

"And Fitch declared that his sister croaked last year," Badger threw in. "One reason you make it official is to get access to their belongings."

"Next of kin," I finished for him.

One question partially answered only succeeded in spawning several more to replace it. Our attempts to unravel this crisscross of relationships led to the same place—a vague trail pointing back east and disappearing on the horizon leading to the desert.

"Maybe that detective in Phoenix can fill some stuff in for us," I offered.

"As long as the Alzheimer's hasn't kicked in," Badger scoffed.

Badger often felt threatened when anyone trespassed on his turf, but I ignored his snub and placed a call on speaker. Detective Fortin was a key link in this story and we needed his help. He answered on the third ring.

"I'm mad at you, Mr. Restic."

"Why's that, sir?" I said into the conference phone.

"Because you got me thinking about work again," he answered. "I'm supposed to be retired."

"Enjoy the rest of your life," Badger threw out.

"What's that?" Fortin asked.

"Nothing," I answered, and shot Badger a look. "I got the sense you rather enjoyed your work."

"Love-hate, more accurate," he said. "Cost me a family, among other things. I'd rather not have it cost me my retirement, too."

I thought about that statement and momentarily got lost in an evaluation of my own life's work. I struggled with the passion he expressed, not because I didn't think it was sincere, but because I had so little for mine. While the detective's career-long struggle was that of never finding the right work-life balance, I grappled with the question of whether I could remain in such a state of indifference about my career for forty years.

"I'm having a hard time hearing you," I said. There was a fair amount of background noise coming through his line.

"That's my retirement," he said. Detective Fortin explained he was on his way to the mountains for a week's worth of fishing and drinking.

"Alone?"

"Is there any other way?"

"I'm just looking for some more information on Maggie Fitch," I said. "I think I found her."

The only response I got was the road noise from his phone. The detective ember still burned. I let him stoke it for a while in silence.

"Good ole Maggie," his voice whistled.

"The one who got away," Badger quipped.

"Oh, I got her," he shot back. "I just never had her mounted on my den wall."

I asked the detective a series of clarifying questions about Maggie's arrest and subsequent disappearance. I was particularly interested in how she made bail, given that it was such a large sum. I purposely ignored Badger's gaze, knowing it was his idea in the first place.

The detective answered some of my questions half-heartedly. The rest he ignored. He was clearly distracted, but it was the good kind of distraction.

"Did he fall asleep?" Badger whispered to me.

Over the speakerphone, we heard the car noise slowly die down. There seemed to be some movement and then the noise picked back up again.

"What are you doing?" I asked.

"You know what I'm doing," he replied.

"Having a stroke," Badger said under his breath.

"How long will it take you to get out here?" I asked with a smile.

"Give me a day or two to collect some stuff back in Phoenix then I'll look you up in La La Land."

COLOR OF SUCCESS

There were two distinct groups among the sixty or so people who showed up to the memorial service at the Palos Verdes house, but neither came to honor Julie.

The executives freely roamed the compound like a long-term houseguest who is overly comfortable in someone else's home. Most looked a little miffed that access to the Dojo was blocked off by stanchions. "Lots of great memories," I overheard Pat Faber remark to another C-suite member as they stared down the long corridor leading to the scene of the crime. Precious recollections of company-funded development sessions would have to wait.

Manning the fringes and clogging up the doorways were the Executive Coaches, Leadership Gurus, Productivity Mavens, and Success Mindset Experts. The coaches mostly talked over each other about the numerous "breakthroughs" their programs/books/

seminars/webinars were delivering. All these projections of success didn't seem to manifest themselves monetarily, though. Their clothes were a little shabby and foreshadowed the sensible compact cars with 150K miles waiting for them down the road and out of sight of the executives' luxury sedans.

The room had correctly sized me up for what I was—a mid-level manager of little significance. I fell short of the status needed to garner the resentment of other executives but not high enough to get the attention of the coaches looking to land another gig. In this realm of the undesirables, I was able to witness the depressing event in peace from the comfort of an armchair.

There was no memorializing of the deceased—Julie's name was almost never mentioned—and there were no condolences offered to the deceased's widow; Rebecca was just a stranger in her own home as she hung around the cheese table. In a simple black shirt and pants, she looked more like one of the caterers than the chief consolee. The few times someone paid their respects to her occurred after they'd shoved a block of smoked gouda in their mouths only to realize the person giving them the napkin was the bereaved party.

The memorial somehow managed to outdo the most insincere of celebrations: the office birthday party. The vapid conversations were that much emptier. The political maneuvering was that much more obvious. Executives one-upped each other with plans for ski vacations, and the coaches jostled each other in the hallway leading to the bathroom so they could

be the first to give their elevator pitch to anyone waiting in line.

I had feared the memorial would be a sham but I
wasn't ready for this version of it. Rebecca had taken
the call from the Palos Verdes police informing her that
the extensive search of the vast shipping port below the
Vincent Thomas Bridge (for a body that wasn't there)
was sufficient to officially declare Julie dead. Rebecca
surprised me by immediately organizing a service. As
I sat there watching the display in front of me, I tried
to figure out her motivation but couldn't come up with
anything plausible.

"Meditating?" a voice asked.

Bronson Thibideux sat down next to me. He apparently didn't deem it necessary to darken his attire for
the occasion, but his assistant hovering nearby more
than made up for it as she was dressed like a twice-wid-
owed Sicilian grandmother. The only thing missing was
a black veil. She looked a little unsure of her role at that
moment, particularly whether she should sit down and
join us. Bronson helped clear up the confusion.

"I thought I saw them laying out a pouch of Long
Jing tea," he said. "Be nice on a cold day like today."

It took her a second to grasp what she was being
told. It actually took longer than a second and required
Bronson to shoot her a look that told her to scram.

"Why don't I brew a pot," she chirped, and immediately set off on her errand. That left me and Bronson
to discuss whatever it was he had on his mind. But he
decided to let me lead.

"The consultant community made a good showing," I said, looking out at the gathering.

"They came for the free food," Bronson replied. "It looks more like a Fleecing Expo at the Convention Center than a memorial."

"These are *your* people," I said.

"Not *my* kind," he shot back.

Unlike his fellow consultants skulking on the fringes of the crowd, Bronson confidently trolled the executive turf. He swapped stories like a member of the club. Judging from the quality of his clothes, I was certain he had no need to park his car down the road, far out of sight of any of the executives' judging eyes.

"What were you doing snooping around that house in Burbank?" he asked. That caught me off guard and I struggled to find a response. He filled the void with another question even more direct than the first: "And why the hell did you call the police?"

Bronson was a little too comfortable and casual in his line of questioning, especially when factoring in what happened to Hearns.

"I thought the police might be interested in the man you left for dead in the garage," I answered in a tone that matched his.

"I had nothing to do with that," he said firmly.

Even if true, there was still the fact that Bronson did nothing to help the man. As if sensing my scorn, he added, "They were all in on it."

"In on what? And who is they?"

"You tell me," he replied. "You seem to know just

about everything."

This commenced a five-minute sparring match in which we tried to out-deflect each other. I found myself answering more of his questions than he answered of mine and suddenly wished the flunkey would hurry back with that tea. I had the feeling we might not see her for a while.

"What were *you* doing in Hearns's house?" I asked, trying once again to get the focus back on him. "I left that detail out in my account to the police but could easily recollect it."

"And maybe you could recollect for them why you were in the house, too."

"I'm trying to help Rebecca clear her wife's name," I said, feeling the need to explain. "We don't think Julie murdered Lois or the man they found in Sierra Madre."

"But what do *you* think?" he asked, picking up on the collective "we" that people like to use when they want to hide. "No one ever thinks their loved one is capable of such a horrific crime."

The only way to win this game was to stop playing and say nothing. Apparently Bronson was as uncomfortable with silence as the rest of us and decided to fill it. "I wouldn't be surprised by anything about Julie," he said. "She's rotten."

I wondered how much he knew. It was possible he knew as much or more than I did about her true identity.

"I broke into the house to recover a document. Julie screwed me on a deal with that 'artist' and I'm trying to undo it. Given all that's going on I could just let it go, but I thought it might be better to clean it up myself."

"Why did you agree to purchase Power of One?" I asked.

That at least got him to stop gazing out at the executive-and-coach waltz playing before us. He looked at me more like a respected adversary than the peon who was thirsty for his wisdom.

"It was a mistake that I'm trying to undo."

"How much money are we talking about?"

"Money for what? The company? It's not much," he said, answering his own question. "It's the reputation risk that matters." He waved his hand at the surroundings. "And I can't let all this...*silliness* besmirch my name."

There existed countless words to describe the events of the past week and yet he chose that one. It was a surprisingly candid explanation told in an unnervingly ho-hum way.

"I stole back what was stolen from me," he said. "No harm, no foul."

He began to look bored with the whole thing. With a tiny attention span, Bronson was more executive than coach and signaled that he wanted to move on to another topic.

"I look forward to working with you on some programs," he told me. There were a lot of assumptions in that statement, namely that he would be granted the contract with my firm.

"We'll do our due diligence and see where we land," I answered in a way that promised nothing and if anything, signaled to him that he should be prepared for an unsatisfactory outcome.

"We'll see," he said in a patronizing manner. He all but patted me on the head and called me "cricket."

I stewed and let the conversations around us fill the silence. One to my right involved a particularly shrill coach bemoaning the new healthcare requirements and recent minimum-wage hikes burdening her small business. The costs of cut-rate insurance and a barely livable wage apparently inhibited her ability to deliver her new program.

"And which one is that?" Bronson challenged.

The coach studied him warily. Bronson had a penetrating gaze that made you question everything you were about to say.

"An eight-week seminar on achieving 'Dignity at Work'?" she replied, more as a question than anything else.

"'Dignity.'" He smiled. Bronson then turned back to me. "Who do you think they're helping?" he asked cryptically and loud enough for anyone nearby to hear.

I glanced around, sensing the awkwardness of the moment.

"I don't understand the question," I deflected.

"All of these people," he gestured. "Who are they helping?"

I felt the impending cruelty in the answer to that question, meted out on the gurus surrounding us. I decided to make light of the whole thing.

"Oh, I don't know…maybe a bunch of insecure

executives with enormous egos who have over time convinced themselves they deserve what they've been given but every now and then need reminders of how special they are. There's big money in that."

Bronson smiled. The gurus exhaled.

"How long did it take you to write that out?" he asked.

"Been giving it some thought lately."

"Well, you're half right," he said, and leaned in to whisper. "Most of these folks are attracted to this trade for personal reasons." Bronson waved his hand at the people around us. I followed his hand and surveyed the small group of off-the-rack shirts and pantsuits that purported to project professionalism but in reality did the opposite. "They're damaged people channeling their own weaknesses into a program to help others overcome that which they can't. Their greatest success comes from the work they do with themselves."

"Well, it's a good thing you have that Chroma-Map doodad to give you so many insights into the human mind," I said, smiling.

"Chuck," he said, patting me on the knee, "I don't need some dumb tool to tell me what I already know about people."

As Bronson stood up and glided over to collect the cup of green tea waiting for him, I was convinced that had he actually been wearing his Chroma-Map, it would have been pure black.

The memorial was over not long after it started. Executives drifted out in dribs and drabs, and once that pool was depleted, the leadership gurus left en masse. All that remained were the catering folks with thousands of dollars' worth of food destined for the dumpster.

Rebecca and I stood in front of the long gas fireplace built into the living-room wall. The blue gas flame flickered through white stones. You had to all but put your hands on the glass to feel any heat.

"I'm done, Chuck."

I turned back to face her.

"Done with what?"

"All of it," she answered. "The whole search."

"For Julie?"

She nodded, and I finally started to understand, at least partially, Rebecca's decision to hold a memorial for someone still alive—it was a way for her to apply an ending that had so far eluded her.

"Call it what you want," she said. "Energy, heart, desire, need—I don't have enough of any of them to continue looking for someone who'd rather not be found. This is the part where someone suggests it might be better if she were actually dead," she added. "Goddamn..." she faltered, "that doesn't help a bit."

"I'm sorry," I said, continuing my tradition of conjuring up hollow words at the very worst time.

"People like to apologize for things they didn't do," she said, "but rarely for the things they actually did."

For some reason, she then related a conversation about me she'd had with Julie years ago. "She explicitly instructed that you were never, under any circumstance, to get an invite to the Dojo. You were permanently *persona non grata*."

"I knew it!" I said, vindicated that my feelings of exclusion weren't those of an overly insecure person. "I have to admit, I sort of wanted to go."

"Trust me, you weren't missing much."

We rehashed memories from working together while the catering crew folded up the tables. It felt like both of us were delaying something. After some time, while the last of the racks of glassware were wheeled out the front door, Rebecca announced:

"I'm having surgery on Thursday."

I had the urge to make a physical connection, something as simple as squeezing her hand or placing my arm around her. But I did neither. We stood side by side with our backs to the fire and said nothing. Rebecca seemed at peace or just plain exhausted with everything. In either case, it sounded like she had found some level of comfort.

"What a sorry excuse for a fire," she said.

AFTER HOURS

I took surface streets into work, not from a need to skirt traffic, but because it was better to see if I was being tailed. This time, however, I actually wanted to be followed.

I thought I caught a glimpse of it on San Fernando as I wound under the 110 Freeway. When I turned onto Pasadena Avenue and then the bridge over the river, I spotted it again a few cars back. I came up through Chinatown and instead of heading to the office, I drove to Echo Park to Badger's "office."

I fumbled with the parking meter and used the time to survey the street. There was no sign of the car and not much foot traffic other than an occasional homeless man emerging from the park. Making my way down the sidewalk toward Badger's office, a voice called out from one of the storefront vestibules.

"Pretend to look interested in the store," it commanded.

"Huh?" I said, and turned toward the voice.

"Don't look," it commanded.

"Badger?" I asked, recognizing the voice.

I had ruined whatever clandestine meeting arrangement he had planned, so he hastily grabbed my coat and guided me into the vestibule next to him.

"Why are you out here?"

"We have a problem," he stated.

"What happened to the money?" I asked, immediately jumping to that as the source of the issue.

"Nothing's happened," Badger said, gesturing back toward his office. "It's safe and sound." That put my mind at ease, until he added, "I count it every morning to make sure."

My vision of Badger "counting" the money didn't include an accountant's green eyeshade as much as it did him rolling around on mounds of cash in a state of half-dress on the army cot that he called his bed. I just hoped none of it was misplaced during his daily ritual.

"Then what's the problem?" I asked.

"We have a visitor," he said, and pointed through the glass to a car parked down the road with the engine running. A lone figure sat at the wheel. Badger then casually revealed the gun he had under his coat.

"Relax," I said. "I told him to meet me here."

I walked across the street toward the idling car. The driver got out to greet me.

"Detective Fortin?"

We shook hands. He was taller than me and reeked of cigarette smoke. His cop mustache was almost full gray and didn't look like it had been groomed since he retired.

"Thanks for coming out. This is Badger—" I said, but realized he was still lurking in the vestibule. "*That* is Badger," I corrected, and waved in his direction. "Let's go inside."

We sat at a table rescued from a school supply surplus depot and I brought everyone up to speed on everything that had transpired. There was immediate tension between the two "cops" on the single set of turf. But Detective Fortin seemed oblivious to it. Or he justifiably didn't feel the need to be in competition at all.

"Did anyone follow up on the Florida lead?" he asked innocently, which Badger took as a direct assault on his character.

"Of course we did," Badger replied, annoyed at having to answer the question in the first place. "She never left California."

I filled in all of the necessary details that Badger was disinclined to share. The search for the librarian named Julie St. Jean came up empty in Florida. Badger couldn't uncover a single record of her ever having lived there, except for the original documentation of her early life that he had already discovered. The likelihood that she'd moved out of the Sierra Madre home and returned to her birthplace was less likely than it had been.

"We'll probably never know the specifics of what happened to her," I concluded, "but we're pretty sure that the woman who took her name also took her life."

"Why didn't you follow up on that charity?" Badger

threw out.

It was unclear what charity he was referencing and to whom the question was directed. Detective Fortin and I shared a look.

"Which charity?" he asked.

"The one that posted Maggie's bail."

I watched Detective Fortin shift uncomfortably, but it wasn't because of the steel surplus chair. A seemingly small detail in the story of Maggie Fitch and her arrest on a major distribution charge was her ability to post bail, no small feat for someone living on the streets at the time. The hefty sum a charity put up for her release should have, at a minimum, drawn suspicion.

"It was a…curious development," Detective Fortin stammered.

"Did you know who was behind the charity?" Badger asked.

"We did." After a pause, he added, "And you would like to know why we didn't have someone tail Maggie after her release."

"Not my place to question the work," Badger said, but everyone knew he was doing just that.

"I appear to be the only one in the dark," I said, trying to ease the tension. "Can someone please fill me in?"

Detective Fortin deferred to Badger. "You seem to have a good grasp of what happened."

It must have been complicated because this time Badger pulled out actual sheets of paper. His documentation consisted mostly of internet printouts of newspaper articles with notes scratched in pencil in the margins. This was an impressive feat given that Badger didn't own a computer. He had printed the articles on the backs of fliers posted at his local library. The colored sheets still had pinpricks in them from where tacks had once held them to the corkboard.

"Phil Arturo," he announced.

"No idea who that is," I answered. Badger was trying his hand at a dramatic unveiling and neither I nor Detective Fortin had the patience to oblige him. "Let's keep it moving. Who is Phil Arturo?"

"He was a real estate developer in Phoenix back in the eighties. He did planned communities but on the cheap side. Glorified trailer parks," Badger said, sniffing. I let it pass that his current residence could only dream of being elevated to "trailer trash" level. "It wasn't a bad business, made decent cash."

"But?" I prodded.

"But Arturo ran around like he was Timmy Tycoon."

Badger listed off all the clichés of the newly wealthy—vacation homes, sports cars, boats. And the kind of things you never stop paying for—prostitutes and drugs.

"When the last of the money went up his nose he came up with a new idea and a new buyer: the savings and loans."

I recalled the scandal that rocked the financial industry and sent the country into a recession. The thrifts were in a pickle. They borrowed money at one rate and lent it out at a lower rate. That unsound practice forced them to find ways to make up the difference. The answer was to invest it, but all that did was move them further out on the risk spectrum, well past the point of "risky" and fully into "you're a buffoon" territory.

"Arturo was their guy," said Badger.

He continued: Arturo promised outsized returns on short lock-up periods. The too-good-to-be-true investment was far worse than that phrase implied. He was running a Ponzi scheme in which he paid old investors with new-investor money. The money moved from hand to hand but where it never went was into an actual investment.

"Then it ended," Badger said..

The wave couldn't go on forever and it came crashing on shore. When new S&L money dried up, so did the source to pay the old S&L folks. That's when the investigators came knocking.

Badger slid a printout across the table. It was a photograph he had pulled off an old article on Arturo. Not the best of pictures but good enough for me to recognize the face.

"The guy in the Cadillac," I said.

"He's here?" Detective Fortin asked.

Arturo hadn't changed much over the years. He'd kept his bowling ball physique and apparently never had hair. I couldn't tell but it looked like he still wore the same gold necklace from the 1980s.

"No mistaking him," I said, and tried to make sense of all the new information. "You knew about Arturo?"

"He was well known to our department," Detective Fortin replied. "For all the reasons just outlined."

He turned to Badger. "Nice work, son."

Badger finally got the recognition he so coveted, and it was even more special coming from the retired investigator. He pretended to shrug it off.

"Listen," began the speech, "it's what I do—"

"Yeah, I know," I quickly jumped in. No one was in the mood for an ego-stroking session, particularly the old detective who looked a little sullen at having his deficiencies in detection exposed. The last thing this newly formed team needed was two sulkers who felt underappreciated. I got us back to the details of the case. "So how does this connect to Maggie?"

"The charity was a women's advocacy group run by Arturo's wife," Detective Fortin explained "and funded with Arturo's money. As far as anyone could tell, the only contributions they made toward their advocacy cause were throwing fancy galas where a few ladies of ill repute were in attendance."

"So they were a sham," I said.

"More than that. Once the Ponzi party ended the Feds went straight for the charity." It was the first mention of the FBI getting involved, and the way the detective mentioned them, I assumed the involvement was unwanted. "That's where they thought the money was hidden."

Authorities recovered only a fraction of the money stolen by Arturo and his investment scheme. Large amounts were unaccounted for—even factoring in the portion that went up his nose, it should have been several million dollars.

I feared Badger might divulge the fact that over two million in cash was sitting in boxes just behind the dusty curtain. But he never brought it up, and I assumed he shared my concern over how our handling of the money might come across to a longtime law enforcement officer.

"So the Feds jacked up your case," Badger surmised.

"Yup," nodded the detective.

"Figures," he commiserated, and in that instant, Badger and Detective Fortin formed a bond over a mutual enemy.

"So the wife had to be in on it with Arturo from the start," I riffed.

"Maybe," Detective Fortin replied. "We'll never know. She was murdered."

Karen Arturo's body was found in the desert by a couple of hikers a month after her charity posted Maggie's bail. Her body was badly mutilated and partially burned and left for the elements and animals to do their damage.

"What a mess," Detective Fortin shuddered. "Couldn't even tell it was her."

The scenario the police developed involved Arturo and Maggie concocting some plan to run off with whatever money remained. Arturo's wife got wind of it and thus became a threat that had to be removed.

"We tried to hang it on Arturo."

"Tried?" I asked with trepidation, knowing what was coming.

"Couldn't make it stick. We had a rock-solid motive and no evidence. Feds eventually got him on fraud, among other things. Thirteen years," he said and whistled. "He'd still be in if I'd gotten him."

"Redemption time," Badger said, and patted the detective on the knee in a surprisingly tender gesture.

That seemed to lift the old man's spirits.

"So how do we find Maggie?" he asked.

SMOKE OUT

etective Fortin's redemption would have to wait a few days. Despite our shared desire to bring Maggie/Julie in, I had a personal reason that superseded whatever justice he wanted to mete out.

We set a time for the next day for the three of us to regroup, giving Detective Fortin time to find a reasonable hotel room. As soon as he was gone, I turned to Badger.

"I'm going to need those boxes."

"Which boxes?" he asked.

"With the money."

Badger blanched.

My suspicion that he was using the money for extracurricular activities suddenly felt much more severe, like maybe those activities involved him spending it. But as we pulled away the tarp that covered the boxes and lifted a lid, I saw all the bills there in their stacks.

"How'd it get so wrinkled?" I asked.

"Maybe when we transported it over here," he said sheepishly.

Badger and I made an elaborate display of loading the Power of One boxes into my car. All along, it felt like someone was monitoring my activities, and I wanted to leave no doubt that I was in possession of the money. I drove over to the office and then made an equally elaborate show of unloading the boxes in front of my building and wheeling them into my office.

Then I waited.

I waited for everyone to leave for the day, which was pretty much accomplished by 4:55 p.m. Then I waited for the cleaning crew to pretend to dust and run a vacuum over the spotless carpet. And then I waited for someone to come for the Power of One boxes.

I heard the click of the electric doors sometime before 3 a.m. Sitting in a cubicle a few doors down from my office, I watched a figure comfortably make its way down the darkened hallway toward me. The figure went straight for my office and stopped in front of the boxes that I had left on the table.

"Need some help?" I asked, coming in behind her and flicking on the overhead light.

"If you have to ask," Julie replied, "then I assume you had no intention of giving any."

"Probably not."

"It's good to see you, Chuck."

"You missed your memorial," I said. "It was a nice service. Just enough insincere gibberish to honor Julie

St. Jean properly. Or is it Maggie Fitch?"

Her demeanor didn't betray if I had succeeded in surprising her with that pronouncement. Julie just eyed me coolly. I decided to rattle off all of the things I knew about her—the car purchase in Baldwin Park, the drug arrest in Phoenix, the Bakersfield meetings with Lois and her ex-husband, the sale of Power of One to Bronson. The breezy fashion in which I relayed these details had the intended effect of demonstrating that I had many other discoveries to relate. I later realized that despite my assertions that Julie was a fraud, I still had a need to prove myself to her. Like all great manipulators, Julie took advantage of this.

"You always were good at pointing out people's mistakes," she said. "A man's shortcomings manifest in the criticisms of others."

"Was that Gandhi?"

"Pat and I talked about you," she started, "trying to figure out where someone of your makeup should sit in the organization. Pat never had faith and neither did I. Actually, that's not fair. No one gave you much thought."

"I know misplaced confidence is one of your strengths, but given the position you're in now, I'm not sure it's warranted."

I saw her make a slight movement with her right hand in her raincoat pocket, and then I understood why she felt so free to eviscerate me in that moment.

"One other detail I forgot to mention earlier." I motioned to her pocket. "I think you bought more than a jalopy from that skinny fellow in Baldwin Park. I'm sure the Sierra Madre police would like to match that with the bullet they pulled out of Jimmy Fitch."

"I didn't kill him."

"Police think you did. What about Lois?"

"What about her?"

"They think you did that, too."

"I've never killed anyone in my life!" she snapped, then seemed to hesitate.

"Let me guess," I said. "You forgot Karen Arturo."

That jab clearly landed.

"Just give me the money," she said flatly.

"You really think I was dumb enough to leave the money in the boxes?"

"I need that money," she said.

Gone was the bloviating I had come to expect from Julie. In its place were crisp declarations that if not for the content of their message, I'd have found rather refreshing.

"It's somewhere you won't find it."

"You're a fool," she spat, not so much an insult as a warning.

"Probably."

"No, you don't get it," she said, and shifted to a more conciliatory tone. "You got a lot right but you also got a lot wrong, and even more you didn't get at all."

"Enlighten me."

"It's better if I don't," Julie said. "I know that sounds like a cop-out, but it's true. This is deep, Chuck. I was involved in some stuff a long time ago, but it got far worse. It's more than just me."

"Your friend from Arizona?" I asked.

Julie looked at me like she didn't know who I was referring to. I described him the best way I knew how.

"Is he here already?" she asked nervously, even glancing over her shoulder as if he might be coming down the hallway at that moment.

"What happened?"

"Stay out of it."

"I'm already in it," I explained. "Arturo posted your bail, then you skipped with his money and now he wants it back."

Julie smiled, but it didn't look like she was impressed with my discoveries.

"If only it was that simple," she said wistfully. "You're going to get yourself killed, Chuck. I'm the least of your concerns right now." To punctuate the point, she revealed the gun that I had assumed all along was in her pocket and waved it casually. "Just give me the money and go play somewhere else."

The words were more threatening than the gun.

"Okay," I agreed.

"Where is it?" she said, sighing, relieved to finally put an end to my meddling. Her victory was short-lived.

"Sorry, that's not the deal."

I watched her calculate how big a cut I was going to demand. It pleased me that the leadership guru was so poor at discerning my motivations.

"I don't want any of the money," I continued. "You can have it all, no questions asked, no cops, nothing."

She waited for the demand.

"You have to meet with Rebecca first."

"How is she?" she asked, her bravado suddenly deflating.

I thought of many retorts to her sudden concern for Rebecca but opted for the truth instead. "She's sick."

I waited for an impassioned defense of her actions or maybe even a sign of contrition. Instead, I got insulted.

"You always were such a one-dimensional thinker," she hissed.

"I don't even know what that means," I said, laughing. "Neither do you."

It took all my restraint to not call the police at that very moment. But I resisted because I knew I would never hold up my end of the deal. Julie would get the money, all right, but she'd also get greeted by the cops as soon as Rebecca had been able to see her.

"Better do it fast," I told her, and made a move for the door. "Rebecca's having surgery on Thursday."

A NEEDLESS EXCHANGE

Everything about the place said mid-tier hotel hoping to be something more: the valet loop and couldn't-be-bothered attendants, the four-story atrium with glass-capped ceiling, the chain coffee shop, the potted palms and ivy-stuffed planters where hidden speakers pumped classical music into the echoing lobby. But something was off.

Hotels don't have security guards. The gift shop was three times bigger than it needed to be. The few patrons milling about had no luggage. And the clearest signal that we weren't where it seemed was the age of the front-desk receptionist. Pushing seventy, she was the last person you wanted greeting guests if your ultimate goal was to project a contemporary image. But she was perfect for the role she held.

She led us into a warmly decorated room where a hospital bureaucrat calmly walked Rebecca through a series of documents and legal disclaimers that indemnified the organization and staff from potential lawsuits. Neither side believed they prevented anything, but Rebecca signed them anyway.

She then made the handoff to an admittance nurse who outlined the process awaiting Rebecca. They adhered to a classic communication tactic for difficult situations: tell them what is about to happen, do it, then remind them of what just happened. There was comfort in believing you knew what was going on.

The admittance process then consisted of a series of check-ins with various nurses, each stage involving us going deeper into the core of the building, where the scrubs gradually changed color, the doors became more hospital-like, and all natural light disappeared. The one thing that didn't change was the tone of the people we met along the way. Cheerful but impersonal, which I assumed was their way of coping. The old ones almost never looked Rebecca in the eye. They didn't last this long by becoming too involved.

The final room was a holding pen of sorts where patients waited to be called into the pre-op room. Up until that point, there was a constant stream of questions and instructions and small tasks to distract from the real reason for the visit. But in this room all of that ended and the minutes dragged on in relative quiet. It was the ideal setting to dwell on the thing neither of us verbalized—the fact that Julie never showed.

Rebecca and I had spent the previous night pretending as if we weren't waiting, but that's exactly what we did. Any sound outside—the hollow drum from water dripping in the downspouts or my neighbors driving by on their way home—immediately pulled our attention away from whatever we were doing to give a hopeful glance outside. I even came up with a reason to leave the back slider unlocked and to disable the sensor lights around the house just in case someone wanted to visit us and preferred a shroud of secrecy.

But Julie never came.

The passing hours dimmed whatever chance we had that she would show. For no logical reason, I felt like I had let Rebecca down.

Rebecca finally accepted it wasn't going to happen. "You going to start a fire?" she asked.

"You should really try to get some sleep," I suggested.

She looked like she was going to pass out but she also lingered by the hearth like someone in need of something. I built a fire mostly out of kindling and sticks and one or two very small logs. It was the kind of preparation that made for a very brilliant but very fast burn. The room lit up almost instantly. We stood in front of the hearth and watched the yellow flames disappear high up into the flue.

Rebecca called it a night a few minutes later. The fire didn't last much longer after that.

I decided to wait back in the main lobby. The room I was allowed to occupy just didn't feel right. Filled with nervous spouses, nervous siblings, and in one instance, nervous parents, the room made me start to feel unworthy of the company it kept.

I ordered a coffee and sat on one of the handful of couches in the grand atrium. I put a call in to Badger to get an update.

"Where are you?" I asked. I had a hard time hearing him over the background noise.

"Out on the street," he shouted. "Jerk-off valet wouldn't let me hang in there with my car. Said I had to shut off my engine."

Badger explained that his car had been acting up and it was better to keep it running because otherwise he was afraid he'd be unable to start it again. The fact that Badger even owned a car surprised me. I didn't think he had the finances to afford one and instead did all his detective legwork using LA's woeful public transportation system. Access to his own wheels somewhat diminished my respect for his bloodhounding. But I needed him and his car this time. Naively hoping Julie would show, I had him waiting outside the hospital with the money.

"Any sightings?" I asked.

"Haven't seen her."

"Okay, hang tight…" my words drifted as I hung up the phone.

I stared out the front at the line of cars in the valet loop. The drop-offs came in from the left and the pickups pooled on the right. And in between, one car was granted an exception.

The old-man Cadillac parked wherever the hell it wanted to.

"You like it?" asked the voice.

Arturo stood behind me and placed a hand on my shoulder.

"Let's go for a ride," he suggested.

With one hand in his pocket on the gun I assumed was inside, there wasn't much room for debate. As we walked out, I eyed the armed security guard manning the front entrance. I kept my gaze on him, waiting for eye contact so I could engage. I just needed an opening so I could alert him of Arturo carrying a firearm on the premises. But the man was interested only in monitoring passing women's derrieres. Arturo guided me out.

"Hey bud," he called out to the security guard and walked us over in his direction. "Where can we get a *real* coffee? Not this overpriced bullshit these guys are slinging!"

We lingered there for a minute while Arturo and the guard swapped jokes, then another minute while the guard thought of a place for us to go. Address in hand, Arturo went out front and slipped some bills to the valet captain. He looked back at me. I could easily have waved him off and headed back inside but everything seemed so casual. It was silly at best, bordering on outright rude, not to join him. So I jumped in the car.

"Do you trust that dope?" he asked, as we pulled out of the hospital complex.

My mind immediately raced. Unclear what dope he was referencing, I wanted to string him along to learn what I could.

"Probably don't have a choice," I replied vaguely.

"Huh?" he said. "We've passed five coffee shops already and he's sending us to the boonies."

I realized the dope Arturo referenced was a human being, the chatty security guard back at the hospital.

"Guy looked like he drinks his out of Styrofoam," he said, laughing. "Probably a treat when he can get one of those flavored creamers. Daily Grind," he said. "Never trust anyone who uses puns."

Later, I understood what he was referring to but in the moment I had no idea what he was talking about. Arturo's preferred communication style was the run-on sentence. He strung disparate thoughts together without the clear breaks needed to alert his listeners that he was on to a new topic. If visually represented, it would look like one single-spaced paragraph with no punctuation. Only when we had settled in at a shop near the community college did I realize the Daily Grind referred to the coffee shop recommended by the guard.

"Coffee shops are the new homeless hangout," he said, gesturing to a disheveled man taking advantage of the shop's free Wi-Fi. "Where's the money?"

This time I was tracking him. Despite Arturo counting the change just given to him by the barista, I knew what money he was actually talking about. But I pretended I didn't.

"Which money?"

"My money," he clarified. "Let's sit over there. That guy stinks to high heaven," he said, gesturing to the homeless man. We grabbed seats at a small table. "We'll figure out a way to make it amicable. How bad is she?"

Arturo jumped from a potential resolution involving the money to a concern for Rebecca's well-being.

"It's pretty serious," I said.

"Cancer?"

I nodded.

"That fucking disease." He shook his head in frustration. "You been able to find her?"

I assumed the "her" was Julie but I wasn't sure how much information I should give Arturo and tried to deflect.

"It hasn't been easy," I said.

"But you found her."

"We spoke."

"About?"

"What do you think?" I tried.

"When I think, I get into trouble," he said. "Crazy, right?" He then called out to a newly arrived customer shaking the rain off her coat. "I thought Los Angeles was supposed to be a desert. She's been hard to find," he said back to me.

"Very hard."

"I've been looking for twenty years. But you found her in a week. You seem like a smart guy, Chuck, but not that smart. Maybe she found you," he pieced together. "Because you have something she wanted."

Arturo's claim that he wasn't the thinking type wasn't entirely accurate.

"You have the money," he concluded. "Did you give it to her?"

"No," I told him. "We made a deal. As of forty-five

minutes ago she's yet to keep her end of the bargain."

"They been together a long time?" he asked. Arturo was trying to fill in the gaps about the other side of the bargain I had made with Julie for the money. He got to it quickly. "And she never showed. Typical." Arturo found a moment of solace in his cup of coffee. "You ever been betrayed, Chuck?"

I thought of my ex-wife and the time leading up to our separation. As painful as it had been, it didn't feel quite at the level to which Arturo's question seemingly referred.

"I felt betrayed," I answered, "but she didn't betray me."

"I've been betrayed. We had a lot of good times together," he said, drifting. "You were probably too young to enjoy the eighties."

"I was in high school. It was pretty fun...."

"*Really* enjoy the eighties," he appended. "Stupid fun. It was what it was," he said with a shrug.

I sort of appreciated that he didn't layer on a bunch of put-on remorse thirty years after the fact. I felt an acknowledgment that he screwed up and paid for it. But he spared me the self-flagellation you usually hear from the reformed. I had always thought the wallowing in past deeds was one part remorse and three parts reliving the good times.

"Maybe you give me the money," he suggested.

"Why would I do that?"

"Because it's mine."

"You don't want that money, it's too dirty," I said lamely.

"I don't know what that means."

"It'll just get you in trouble again."

"You know about me?" he asked.

"Some things."

"I don't care about the money, Chuck. I just want whatever's going to lure that rat out."

"She double-crossed you," I said.

"I take back that part about you being smart. Those ears don't work so good. Haven't you been listening? Not double-crossed, betrayed."

"I didn't know there's a difference."

"You would if it happened to you." Arturo rose from the table. "Let's go back to the hospital and get that money."

"It isn't there," I said, half-lying. It was there but not in my car.

"Sure it is. How else would you have paid your end of the bargain?"

This time Arturo was less accommodating. He made me walk out first while he followed close behind, in case I decided to make a break for it.

"You drive," he said, tossing me the keys. "Put a scratch on this car and I'll kill you."

As we crossed the parking lot, I heard the squeal of tires and turned to see a battered truck bearing down on me. It looked like one of the thousands of unregistered little Japanese pickups in LA that serve as transportation for two-man landscaping businesses. I had to jump out of its way to avoid being crushed. The car slammed into Arturo's Cadillac and shattered the fin taillight.

"Whoa!" Arturo cried.

The driver door swung open.

"Get in the car, Chuck!" Badger shouted.

Arturo was just now pulling his eyes from the crushed rear end of his true love. He made a move toward Badger, but was stopped by the gun pointed at his chest.

"Why is your landscaper pointing a gun at me?" Arturo asked.

"Do I look like I mow lawns?" Badger asked, annoyed.

"Hey, Badger," I began, "this goes without saying"—which meant it really did need saying—"but let's not do anything stupid."

"Nothing stupid is going to happen because we're getting out of here."

"No one's going anywhere," Arturo announced, "until someone pays for this."

I didn't have any money on me and I knew Badger wouldn't have any. We could have tapped into the millions in the bed of his truck, but that wasn't a good idea.

"I'm sure insurance will cover this," I suggested, but Badger shot me a look that told me maybe not.

"Work's been a little slow," he murmured, "had to make some discrete cuts."

I assumed he meant "discretionary," but how basic car insurance fit into that category escaped me.

I pulled out my cell.

"Who you calling?" Arturo asked.

"The police," I said, "to get an accident report."

It was a toss-up among the three of us who liked that idea the least. Badger could little afford a citation for operating without insurance. Arturo had a natural aversion to law enforcement and was not the type to involve them in anything if he could help it. And I didn't need a long, drawn-out process—I needed to get back to the hospital to check in on Rebecca.

"Or I could pay for it," I suggested.

Arturo caressed the taillight like it was a loyal hound heeling at his side while he mulled over the offer.

"You got the money on you?" he asked.

"No."

He scoffed. But it was the least unpleasant of a long list of unappealing options, so he accepted it, reluctantly. We exchanged cell phone numbers even though he seemed fully capable of tracking me down in case I reneged.

"I'm going to break his neck," he said at the end of the transaction, incapable of addressing the person who was the actual target of the threat.

Badger rightly pretended not to hear him.

My having to pay for the taillight was an unwelcome development, but at least the incident distracted Arturo enough to forget about his initial request. Almost.

"I'm going to need that other money, too" he said, as we parted ways.

Arturo still had a rat to catch.

OFF POINT

During one of the numerous stops before the surgery, Rebecca was asked to provide emergency contact numbers. Instinctively, she put down her home number and Julie's cell number—then realized the issues with that.

"Should I put you down?" she had asked.

The right thing to do wasn't the right thing at that moment.

"Leave it," I said.

Her desire to believe was needed more than any kind of acceptance of the truth.

In the end, several irretrievable messages were left on an answering machine in an empty house and on a smashed cell phone in the bottom of a trash can somewhere near Union Station.

I knew that Rebecca was dead even before the doctor came out to deliver the official message. I had returned to the hospital a few hours after she had gone into surgery and as I approached the desk in the waiting area, there was something in the young nurse's eyes that told me it was over. She scurried off and returned a few minutes later with the doctor in tow.

He spoke about cardiac arrest, resuscitation attempts, and other procedures I only half-understood and half-heard. It was informational but not too clinical. He gave me a few moments to realize I didn't have any questions for him before offering his condolences and returning to work.

It was a pitch-perfect, well-practiced delivery of a message straight out of the handbook, penned in equal measure by grief counselors and legal advisors. And I resented him for so easily and so faithfully sticking to the script.

"We left messages at the contact numbers you gave us," the nurse explained once the doctor had left. She apparently felt the need to address why I had to hear about Rebecca's death like this. "I even went out to the lobby but I couldn't find you. I'm sorry," she said, her voice quavering slightly and her eyes just barely starting to well up before her survival instinct kicked in and she steeled herself to return to work.

That brief display of compassion was enough to give me hope that not everything is a choreographed process to manage expectations. She had fallen prey to an actual emotion and temporarily went off script. That alone gave me enough strength to absorb what was to follow.

I met with another layer of hospital administration

that you see only when tragedy strikes. No next of kin—outside of a wife who was officially dead but in reality a missing person—presented a bit of a quandary for the team. Having probably encountered every scenario over the years, this one was particularly troubling. They couldn't release the body to me because I wasn't named on the admittance form and had no documentation to prove I had any legal authority. It took an entire week to sort it out before I was able to hire a service to deal with Rebecca's remains. Badger's effort to find even a distant third cousin came up empty and in the end, they were granted to no one.

Five days later there was another memorial, this time at my house. The Palos Verdes home had been an option since I had the key among Rebecca's belongings, but I felt uncomfortable pursuing that. Besides, we wouldn't have been able to fill the smallest room there.

No executives showed up, and without them, none of the pilot fish consultant gurus did either. The gathering was a random collection of people who sat on either end of an invoice—pool cleaners, gardeners, house cleaners, and the payroll folks from the various corporations Power of One had worked with.

One additional person was there, but he stayed out of sight just in case Julie got sentimental and decided to show up. I spotted the young detective from Palos Verdes Estates in his car, parked down the road from my house. I pulled up next to him on my way back from the pastry shop.

"Didn't mean for you to come," I told him. "Just

wanted to let you know that Rebecca had passed."
I knew that wasn't the reason for the visit. "Or are you
waiting for someone?"

"Was in the neighborhood," he said.

"She's not going to show," I told him.

"Who's that?"

"The woman who killed Lois Hearns."

"Julie St. Jean didn't kill her," he said.

"No? Who did?"

"We found traces of the deceased's blood—" he
started, but must have picked up my wincing at the excessive use of jargon and decided to speak to me in plain
English. "James Fitch. Her blood was on his clothes."

"Who killed Fitch then?"

"That's for my friends in Sierra Madre to figure out.
I'm only worried about my area of responsibility."

"If that was true, you wouldn't be here."

Although his department had declared Julie dead,
he still had his doubts. I might have underestimated
him, but then again, he was dumb enough to drive all
the way across town to sit in a car all day on the chance
that Julie would actually show up to say goodbye to
Rebecca.

"You going to come in?" I asked.

"Don't want to intrude," he said.

I didn't have the heart to tell him that we could have
used the extra body to help fill out the room.

"If you change your mind, we're just up the road."

Compelled to hold the service for my friend, I bore
the disappointment that so few people had decided to

show. I mercifully brought it to a close fairly quickly. The few folks who'd come filed out and then it was just me, Badger, and Detective Fortin.

Detective Fortin wasted no time verbalizing the question on all our minds.

"Now what?" he asked.

With Rebecca's death, there was no longer the need to search for Julie. The police or Arturo or someone else would eventually track her down. Even the unspoken desire to punish her somehow dissipated with Rebecca's passing. Julie's life was ruined to a point from which even she, the master of reinvention, couldn't recover.

The obvious choice was to walk down the the road and unload everything we'd learned about Julie to the doubting young detective. He had the basic pieces—the affair with Lois, the blackmail scheme, the connection to the murder in Sierra Madre—but he didn't know anything about Julie's past in Arizona, the missing money, or her double life.

But no one seemed very interested in doing that.

I studied the two men in the room with me. I had raised Detective Fortin's hopes for a chance at redemption only to threaten to snatch it away. And Badger just looked like someone who wasn't ready to end his morning "counting" ritual with Julie's money.

"It's the correct thing to do," Badger said.

That got me to smile, because in this instance, Badger's poor word choice was actually appropriate.

"But not the right thing," I added. "Let's go get Julie."

TAP-TAP-TAP

I was convinced I was right until the third day that nothing happened.

I figured a person on the run needs a place to sleep and that simple requirement can be challenging for someone with no access to credit cards or ATMs and probably no cash left. By this point Julie's car had to be a liability. Sleeping in it like the dozens of semi-homeless do near parks wasn't worth the risk when patrols, pressed upon by angry neighborhood committees, constantly came around to scare them away to another spot. She had no loyal relatives with a blinding duty to family that allowed them to overlook the fact that they were hiding a murderer on the run. There was also a small detail I now recalled from when I first followed Rebecca out of the Omni Hotel.

She had led me to the commercial building overlooking the 110 Freeway and, I presumed, had gone upstairs to the unfinished space that was supposed to become Power of One's new headquarters. But then they ran into financial difficulties and had to stop construction. I remembered when Rebecca first entered the building she carried a small bag with her, but when she emerged she no longer had it with her.

I asked my ex-wife to make some calls and get me a tour of the unfinished floor. Claire and I had remained on good terms after the divorce and seemed to forever hover in a space where after a few cocktails I wondered, just maybe, about the viability of a reunion. Morning sobriety always brought back clarity.

Claire was a lawyer in commercial real estate and was pretty well connected to all of the building management companies in downtown Los Angeles. Posing as a potential lessee, I gained entrance to the floor and was able to snoop around—albeit with the building's agent as a chaperone—for any signs of recent activity. I spied the bag Rebecca had left and it looked to be empty but I couldn't be sure. I was already getting the squirrelly eye from the agent for my complete inability to provide details about the alleged tech start-up I'd founded. The fact that I spent the majority of the time examining the detritus of the construction site didn't help build conviction.

Now convinced that Julie was using the place to evade capture, I set a plan in motion. Badger, Detective Fortin, and I took shifts watching the building for any sign of Julie. For practical reasons we limited the work to the hours between six in the evening and six in the morning. I figured if she was using the space to hide out she would likely time her entrances and exits to the hours when as few people were around as possible. We divided the twelve-hour shift among the three of us, which meant four-hour stints sitting in a car, waiting.

We all began as enthusiastic supporters of the idea. Badger, in particular, was the most eager, but then again he was the only one getting paid. I needed to respect the fact that, for me, it was a personal decision to continue the search for Julie, but for Badger, it was still his livelihood and I couldn't deny him that. He cut me a break on his hourly rate and also took the job very seriously. He dressed in all black and came equipped each evening with a giant set of binoculars that could read hedge language off a pharmaceutical ad from a thousand yards away. An empty plastic bottle served as his personal porta-potty.

Since I owned the first shift, there was no need to go home after work because the building was less than a mile from my office. I took advantage of that by firing off as many emails as possible after five o'clock to prove my dedication to the firm. Although I resisted the urge to open the emails with:

You're probably gone for the day....

I did subtly close each one with:

Let's connect when you get back in the office tomorrow....

Solidifying my position as the firm's leading burner of the midnight oil, I'd grab a sandwich on the way out and make the short drive over to the building, where for the next three nights I watched a service entrance on a side street where absolutely nothing happened.

Although two decades of meaningless conference calls conditioned me for prolonged periods of stationary life, this was something different. I didn't have the distractions of someone babbling on about a nothing initiative to lull me into a near hibernation state, where I could slow my heart rate and still be able to throw out "value" comments to hide the fact that I wasn't listening. Instead, it was the wicked combination of silence and my own thoughts that made this a brutal experience.

Counting the minutes in solitude also eroded whatever confidence remained in my theory that Julie was hiding out on the unfinished floor. After the third day, a feeling of dread grew as the hour when Badger relieved me approached. I couldn't bear to see the look on his face—the most enthusiastic of the three of us—as he too started to lose faith.

"Still nothing?" he said. This time he wasn't wearing his customary full-body rain slicker with seaman's cap—an outfit needed only if you planned on standing in the elements all night. He even had a newspaper tucked under his arm.

"Nothing," I confirmed.

Early the following morning I decided to put an end to the wasted effort. I swung by the stakeout building on my way into work to tell Detective Fortin that we needed a new plan.

But he wasn't there.

It was still more than an hour before his shift was technically supposed to end. Perhaps he had come to the same conclusion that I had and decided to call it early. I checked my phone again just in case I'd missed any texts while I was sleeping. The message list was empty.

I didn't think anything of it and went in to work, getting lost in the meaninglessness of a long day of meetings and conference calls. By late afternoon, when my texts to Detective Fortin hadn't been returned, I started to worry and placed a call to Badger.

"I saw him at two this morning," he said.

"Did you hear anything from him after that?"

"No, why? Did he go MIA on us?" he asked acerbically.

Although Badger had ceased antagonizing his "rival," he hadn't exactly grown to respect him. It still showed up in subtle digs at his advanced age and in not-so-subtle digs at his competency.

"Guy probably realized he couldn't hang," said Badger. As if sensing that he had pushed it too far, he shifted to a slightly more conciliatory tone. "You know where he's staying? I could swing by and check up on the poor fellow."

I didn't have an address.

"Let me try a few more times to get him on the phone," I said.

"Should we keep going on the stakeout?"

The detective's disappearance gave me hope that maybe the original idea was correct after all.

"Yeah, let's do one more night."

"Cool with me," he said. "It's your dime."

I wished it was only a dime.

"You want me to take his shift, too?" Badger asked hopefully. I thought I heard him smack his lips.

"Let's split it up," I suggested. "Come by at midnight."

The storms rolled back into the LA basin that afternoon and dropped a steady rain for hours on end. I had to keep a few windows cracked because the humidity in the car kept fogging up the glass, which obscured my view of the service entrance. Dark patches formed on the seats where the rain pooled and soaked into the fabric.

I mimicked the tap-tap-tap of raindrops on my roof by tapping them out with my thumb on the steering wheel. This little game slowly grew stale, then turned maddening as I focused on the sound of rain crackling on the roof that seemingly grew louder the more intensely I listened to it. I tried singing but realized I didn't actually know the words to many songs. Then I just sat there.

"You're watching the wrong entrance," a voice breathed into one of the cracked windows.

I stared into the darkness to my right. A face loomed in the window but was so obscured by shadow I couldn't make out its defining features. The door opened and the car's internal light clicked on.

"Let's go inside," Arturo suggested.

A QUICK EXCHANGE

There was little illumination other than the signs above the elevator doors and the security lights dangling every twenty feet or so from the ceiling in yellow, plastic cages. Commercials playing on the city center's giant screens across the freeway turned the space into a kaleidoscope of ambient light as they rolled from one brand to the next.

"Why don't you call your nut-job friend and have him bring the money," Arturo ordered.

Before coming inside the building, Arturo searched the car and had me open the trunk just in case I had the money with me. He commended me on not being dumb enough to keep it on my person.

"I thought you said you didn't care about the money," I said.

"A guy can change his mind, right? Sorry, man, I wasn't lying before," he felt the need to add. "I really didn't want the money. I'd give it up in a heartbeat as payment for finding her. But you found her without me having to do that!" he said, laughing. "I owe you, though."

"And what are you going to do if she shows?"

"She'll show."

"When she shows, then?"

Arturo picked up on my concern that he might have more sinister motives in mind.

"I've never killed anyone in my life," he said. "And I'm not about to start now."

"What about Fitch?" I asked straight out.

Arturo laughed. "Smart guy, Chuck, but you go off the rails sometimes. Why would I kill Fitch?"

"Because you were angry at him for stealing your money."

"*He* didn't take my money," he corrected, and extended his hand. "Better if I take your phone."

I did as instructed.

"What's that guy's name?" Arturo asked.

"Ricohr," I answered.

It was the only name in my contacts who was in law enforcement. I hoped a random, mysterious text from me late in the evening would pique his curiosity enough to come find me.

"Under R," I said, hoping I hadn't added "Detective" to his name.

"Yeah, I got it," Arturo said. He tapped away on the phone. "You said 'Badger,' right?" He looked up at me with a disappointed gaze. "Come on, Chuck, I thought we were friends. You haven't texted or called that Ricohr character for over a year."

Back in the phone, Arturo went to the activity log from the day Rebecca had entered the hospital. He correctly assumed Badger was the right contact name but there was one number that perplexed him.

"What's this number with the Arizona area code?" he asked. "Who could that be?"

He had stumbled upon Detective Fortin's number. I hadn't yet officially put him into my contacts so it came up as an unknown number. I watched Arturo's mind race with all the possibilities, including one he didn't necessarily want to believe.

"Can't be," he whispered.

My skin prickled.

"You've been calling this number all day," he said. He then went and read the texts I had sent, but they didn't give him the answer he was looking for. "Who is it?"

"Call and find out," I suggested.

I watched Arturo debate whether he should call the number to confirm whatever suspicions he had. I wasn't sure if it was a good thing or a bad thing if he did. I never found out.

"Let me guess, he gave himself the name?" Arturo asked, back on the original topic. "Badger," he scoffed. "Bigger idiot than I thought. You still owe me for the damage to my car," he said, switching back to our original discussion outside the coffee shop. "I'm gonna need to collect on that."

"Take it out of the money when it comes."

"But I'd be paying myself," he said, smiling. "Don't be going off the rails on me again."

Arturo gave me specific instructions on what to say to Badger along with a warning to not deviate or else suffer some unstated consequence.

Badger picked up on the second ring.

"Did she show?" he asked.

"Not yet," I replied, and then asked him to bring the money to the building. There was a long pause as his instincts told him something was wrong.

"Sneeze twice if you're in trouble," he said.

"He wants me to sneeze if I'm in danger," I told Arturo with my hand cupped over the phone.

He snatched it away from me.

"Pal, let's not get all dramatic here. No one's getting hurt unless someone decides to make things difficult. Just bring the money and I'll set us square on the damage to my car. Once I have a chance to talk to her, you guys can call the cops and get the glory of the arrest. I'll be long gone by that time."

Arturo handed the phone back to me.

"I think he's serious, Badger. Let's just do what he wants. We don't need any heroics right now."

Badger reluctantly agreed and hung up.

"Is he going to play nice?" Arturo asked.

"I have no idea." There was something Arturo said that I wanted to confirm. "Did you mean that other part about being long gone?"

"Chuck, I've been honest with you the whole time. I want two things—my money and to see her lying face. You guys—" he started but then corrected himself, "well, maybe just you, want to get back at her for what she did to that woman. You want to see her suffer a little bit, don't you?"

I didn't answer but he knew what I was thinking.

"I'd like to see you get that pleasure."

Badger arrived twenty minutes later and followed Arturo's directions to the letter. The transaction was consummated without words. Badger laid the large bag of money on the floor. There was a brief moment when three guys stared at each other and not at the prize that sat between them. When it came time to leave, Badger backed out of the room while keeping his gaze on Arturo the entire time. Despite this awkward moment, the money was exchanged without incident.

"Now we wait," Arturo said, and sat down on a stack of dry mortar.

For over three hours we sat in silence and watched the ever-changing shifts of light from the billboards across the way. I might have dozed off for a minute or two but couldn't be sure. It felt like a sort of half-dream state anyway, until the elevator doors slid open and Julie walked in. She didn't see us until Arturo rose up, and even then she wasn't sure who was waiting for her.

"Hello, Karen," he said. "Been a long time."

REUNION

Phil?" she exhaled, taking a step back.

"You're not going to run again, are you?"

"I can't believe it's you," she said. "It's really you."

It felt like a reunion of lost love but without all the shrieks of joy, rushing into each other's arms, twirls, and faces cradled in hands. They stood awkwardly facing each other. Julie made the first move and wrapped her arms around him. Arturo stood stiffly.

"It's been too long for hugs," he intoned.

Julie's embrace loosened. She returned to her original spot, a suitable distance for acquaintances.

"I finally found you," he said. Arturo seemed unprepared for the moment he had dreamed of for more than thirty years. "You never said goodbye, Karen."

"I panicked," she explained.

"You had enough time to frame me for your murder. I'd still be in prison if that had actually stuck," he said with a shudder.

For the first time since my quest to ensnare Julie St. Jean, I finally felt like I had her. It had less to do with the physical capture and more with an understanding of this ever-elusive figure who had vexed me for decades.

Each new discovery I had made over the last handful of weeks got me closer to the truth—but never quite close enough. When she was the former librarian from Sierra Madre, her reinvention to a brash leadership coach, while great storytelling, never made much sense. When she was the former drug addict from Phoenix, although it was appealing that her roots began in such sordid circumstances, it still didn't match up to the self-made guru of Power of One. But the wife of a con man, and a con artist herself, who jumped ship when the authorities came knocking, who tried to frame her husband for murder so she could save her own scalp, who stole identities (and possibly lives) while on the run—that was the Julie St. Jean I knew and despised.

To Arturo, she was the woman he'd always known, and, judging by the sadness in his voice, it seemed she was the woman he still loved.

"Shit, Karen, I never thought I'd see you again."

"I know," she replied.

Her two words reminded Arturo of the cold truth about the circumstances of their separation.

"But I was the only one looking."

"Phil, I had to leave. You know what was going on. It was chaos. It wasn't safe."

"All the rats jumped ship. Head rat went first."

"As if you would have done any different," she shot back.

Sensing the contrite approach would lead nowhere, Julie went on the attack. It came naturally to her, and having been on the receiving end many times, it was an area of strength for her.

"I never loved you, Phil," she said. "I thought I did but I was wrong." She left off the apology that usually accompanies that kind of statement. "I only loved one person."

The scene quickly deteriorated into pettiness and personal gripes. I felt like an interloper at the breakfast table when one morning a lifetime of marital disappointments comes to a head over coffee and runny eggs. I just wanted to crawl away. Instead, I drifted out of the room without calling much attention to myself. I worked my way over to the elevator banks and hovered near the engine room, where the hum behind the heavy door somewhat drowned out the voices across the way.

I stood there in the half-light and tried not to focus on the muffled voices. Most of the words were incomprehensible but every so often a few were shouted with clarity so I couldn't help but pick them up. If I'd had my cell phone, I might have called the police or texted Detective Ricohr—yet I felt an odd need to hold up my end of the bargain with Arturo.

But the voices were rising, becoming more heated, and the slurs they slung at each other grew more serious and that much more nasty. At one point I heard Arturo shout something, a single word, over and over. I believe it was: "Again."

Then there was a loud pop. I heard some shuffling and then came two more pops in quick succession. Then silence.

I trained my eyes back to where Julie and Arturo had been standing. I couldn't see any movement against the backdrop of flashing lights from the billboards. There were no more voices either.

I stared up at the light dangling overhead and suddenly felt very exposed. A twenty-five-watt bulb held in yellow plastic was a beacon to whomever had fired the shots and might need to fire more.

A hand gently pressed my forearm then squeezed tightly as I instinctively tried to spin away from it. The grip was firm and slowly pulled me out of the light and down to the floor.

Badger crouched on one knee in the shadows and scanned the room.

"What happened?" I whispered.

He made the quiet sign with the barrel of his gun serving as the index figure in the gesture. He cocked his head from side to side, trying to pick up any sounds beyond our hiding spot, but the hum of elevator engines made that difficult.

I gestured for him to call the police, but Badger gave me a disapproving look. We waited a few more minutes, which felt like twenty, then ventured out of the safety of our hiding spot. I made my way back toward the original spot where Arturo and I had waited. A haze of smoke hovered in the air and, without a running ventilation system, remained there in the hermetically sealed room. The acrid stench prickled my tongue.

As I approached, I saw something on the floor that I might have mistaken for a bag of mortar if I hadn't been looking for a person.

Arturo lay on his side, the bowling ball figure finding a flat enough spot to come to rest. His big belly heaved with sporadic gasps. I bent down to him and placed my hand on his shoulder, while Badger called for an ambulance.

"It's all right," I soothed, "they're coming to help."

Arturo's eyes fluttered open and got a look at his rescuer.

"You betrayed me, too," he wheezed.

UNCOURAGEOUS COURAGE

Phil Arturo died later that morning at Good Samaritan Hospital.

Badger and I were a half-mile away in separate interview rooms at the local precinct. We had more answers than they had questions, and I could see the growing annoyance on their faces. The detectives just wanted to understand what had happened up on the twenty-second floor that led to Arturo being shot, and I kept talking about blackmail schemes, a librarian from Sierra Madre, and a Ponzi scheme from 1980s Arizona.

"Who's the woman you say shot the victim?" the detective asked again.

"Her real name?"

"Any name," he gritted.

"Well…" I began, and watched them wilt.

We forever seek simplicity in the chaos. We want crisp answers to complex things. Sometimes those answers exist but mostly we have to make one up to satisfy the need. I made a career out of doing this successfully but this was one instance when I laid everything out in all its ugly truth. My meddling had gone too far and it was time to show all of my cards and deal with whatever repercussions might come with the reveal.

The police were convinced that we were behind Arturo's murder, and by *we* they really meant Badger, and gave him a good working over. But the gun they found on him hadn't recently been fired and there were no powder burns on him, proving he hadn't fired another gun, either. He had the legal right to carry his gun and there was nothing left to pin on him or me outside of a trespassing charge that the building management had no interest in filing. They, too, wanted nothing more to do with Julie St. Jean and Power of One.

I was relatively fortunate that Badger was the less desirable of the two of us—he had a questionable job and sketchy past and just didn't look presentable—and thus bore the brunt of their efforts. Also, I had a friend on the inside.

"Still playing games?" Detective Ricohr asked as he waddled into the room. "You look like hell."

"I almost called you before all this happened," I told him.

"I'm glad you didn't. Did you do anything stupid?"

"Probably."

"The illegal kind?"

"No, I don't think so."

"Okay, let me see what I can do."

Despite the help, I was held for five hours and all we did was talk. We went through the events over and over again. Once they decided I wasn't a lunatic, they actually started to listen to what I was saying. Soon they were helping me piece together the various parts of the puzzle, though it wasn't until many meetings and several days later that a single narrative came together.

Eventually, the representatives on the cases of the three murders—Palos Verdes Estates and Lois Hearns, Sierra Madre and James Fitch, Los Angeles and Phil Arturo—worked to weave together the entire story. The fourth player—Detective Fortin from Phoenix—was still missing, and his section would remain unfinished until he was found, if ever.

The path that led to the three murders began when Karen Arturo's true identity was revealed. There was a lot of debate among the detectives over the source of that development. One theory had Julie herself divulging the secret to Lois after one of their lovemaking sessions in Sierra Madre. Another had Fitch doing his own research on his murdered sister, like the amateur sleuth who stumbles on something far bigger than he can handle. One outlandish idea was that it came from Bronson Thibideux. Doing his due diligence on the purchase of Power of One, he uncovered Julie's secret and used it as a bargaining chip when negotiating the deal with Lois. Regardless of how the truth came out, it launched a series of events that ended with Arturo being shot on the twenty-second floor of a commercial building overlooking the 110.

The theory was that Lois and her ex-husband, armed with this new information, teamed up with Fitch and together put the squeeze on Julie. Payments were quickly doled out, but these amounted to short-term fixes; the calls for more money wouldn't stop until the well was dry. With Power of One's financial struggles weighing on Julie's ability to pay, she turned to an old source of cash, the money she'd absconded with when she fled Phoenix. While this provided a deep pool to draw from, it alerted Fitch to its existence. His snooping in Arizona in turn alerted Arturo that the woman he thought was dead, the one whose "murder" almost sent him to prison, was actually still alive. Arturo descended on Los Angeles and further complicated an already complex situation.

A falling-out had likely occurred between the Hearns tandem and Fitch, most certainly over the proportion of the split. Some theorized that the split wasn't organic and might have originated with Julie herself. She convinced Fitch to eliminate his business partners and they'd work out a deal together. Fitch kept his end of the bargain by murdering Lois, but then he foolishly believed Julie would uphold her end of the deal. His life came to an end in the Sierra Madre house with a bullet in the back.

At this point, the only thing keeping Julie in Los Angeles was the box of money in the trunk of my car. It was all she needed to flee and reinvent herself, yet again, in another part of the world. Several attempts to recover the cash had ended in failure. She eventually got the money but she had to go through her ex-husband first, and yet another murder was added to her tally.

By the end of it, Karen Arturo, aka Julie St. Jean, was wanted for the murders of James Fitch, Maggie Fitch, and Philip Arturo. She was also a person of interest in the disappearance of Detective Richard Fortin of Phoenix, Arizona. Many believed it was only a matter of time before his name was added to the list of the dead.

I emerged from the precinct a little after five in the morning to the empty, rain-slicked streets of downtown Los Angeles. With no idea of what to do and without a clear head to come up with an answer, I just started walking. I worked my way back toward the freeway in the direction of Bunker Hill. Empty of thoughts, I walked all the way back to my office in a slight drizzle.

I made my way upstairs and poured myself a hot cup of coffee. I downed it faster than I should have and immediately poured another. My shirt was damp and this made the room feel colder than it actually was. The hot coffee did little to counter it. I remained in the break room for some time and then heard movement behind me.

Pat Faber shuffled in with his head down, unaware of my presence.

"Just getting in?" I startled him.

He wasn't used to anyone arriving at the office before him.

"You're in early," he said, but not as a compliment.

I thrust my coffee mug a little too close to his face.

"My third cup!" I announced, to prove just how

early I had come in.

Pat looked at me the way you'd look at the homeless man you encounter on the street at night and need to ascertain if they are deranged or not. He took a half-step back.

I filled him in on the recent developments with Power of One, Arturo's murder, and Rebecca's passing, and all the blood spilled in their wake. It was overwhelming.

"How did we get in so tight with them?" he asked.

"We're going to play that game now?" I retorted.

"What game?"

"Come on, Pat, you know how it happened. You brought them in."

"I understand that, but how did it get this far?"

"And so it starts," I said, exhaling audibly.

Having done this so many times with associates, I saw it coming even before Pat did. This was the part where he convinced me to take the fall for something I didn't do and then actually made me feel responsible for it. Carried to the extreme, it would lead to my voluntary exit from the firm. But there was no need for that.

The prudent path was to play along with the charade—publicly "own" the failure and then under the banner of "lessons learned," casually outline all the factors that were outside of my control that led to the failure. I'd then bravely close with, "regardless of all that, it's on me." This aggressive-passive approach would give me the appearance of the courageous leader without my having to admit that I did anything wrong.

But that was too easy. And prudence wasn't in the

cards after the events of the last several days.

"I'll take the fall," I said.

"Chuck, this isn't about finding blame," he offered, alerting me that this could be very painless if I played along.

"Of course it is."

They'd actually go easy on me, knowing full well that they'd extract a little flesh come bonus time, and it would appear on my review alongside the fraction of a special payout I was supposed to get.

"It's on me, Pat," I declared. "But we all know who's to blame."

A COLD NIGHT IN BURBANK

L et me guess, you want to help me recover the money,"
he said.

Mr. Hearns moved gingerly back to the stool in his
garage. If he hadn't still been recovering from the beat-
ing he took, he might have dished one out on me. I
made the detour to Burbank because there seemed to
be too many loose ends in the narrative the authorities
had built, including the whereabouts of Detective Fortin. Badger had put in some hours on it but came up
empty. One of the few people—alive that is—who could
address some of these unanswered questions was one of
the alleged participants. But first I had to convince him
it was worth talking to me.

"I'm sorry I wasn't honest with you up front," I said.
"I was just trying to find out some information."

"Who are you?" he asked. "Really."

"I guess I'm nobody."

"Everyone's a nobody."

I explained my relationship with Rebecca and why I had pretended to be someone I wasn't. He didn't seem interested in the details or care much that I lied to him.

"So why are you here?"

"Just looking for some answers."

"Ain't got many of those," he said, and offered me a beer, which was his way of saying he would try anyway.

We sat on stools with the portable heater at our feet.

"Who did all that to you?" I asked, gesturing to the marks on his face.

"I thought it was you."

"You know it wasn't."

"Didn't get a look at him. I heard someone in the garage, came out to look, and then got cracked on the head. I never got the light on so I couldn't make them out."

"You sure it was a man?" I asked.

"It better the hell have been," he said, laughing. "It was a dude, trust me on that."

I nodded even though I couldn't make sense of who it might be.

"It wasn't her. I'd have wrung that wrinkly neck if it had been."

Hearns seemed to get lost in reflection.

"Everything all right?"

"I told Lois not to get involved with that lady," he began. There were many interpretations to what kind of involvement he was referencing, but in this instance it was purely the business kind. "I smelled a phony the minute I met her. She talked a lot but she never said anything."

My affinity for Mr. Hearns grew, if for no other reason than because of his apparent ability to see through in a single encounter with Julie what scores of Ivy League–educated executives had failed to over three decades.

"The police believe blackmail was behind everything," I said.

"First those dirty cops think I killed Lo, then they say I'm the mastermind of a blackmailing ring. No one was blackmailing nobody. At first."

Hearns explained the business proposition presented to Lois. There was a pool of money sitting in a bank account in Phoenix that Julie couldn't access but needed. If Lois helped her get the money, "through legal means," Hearns was sure to clarify, she would get a percentage of the total. "You know Lo was a lawyer, right?"

"Yes, I think you said that before." He'd mentioned it a few times, as any proud spouse might. "How much are we talking?"

"Way less than she deserved."

"What'd your wife have to do?"

"The owner of the bank account was dead, apparently. Had been for a long time. Lo had to make it official."

To get access to the money in Maggie Fitch's account, Maggie needed to legally be declared dead. A claim could then be made by the next of kin on her estate's assets. This new detail shed some light on a few murky areas in the police narrative, particularly around the events in Arizona some thirty years earlier.

With the authorities circling Arturo, his wife Karen seized on an opportunity to save her neck. It came in the form of Maggie Fitch's arrest on a drug possession charge. Perhaps Karen knew Maggie from the start or even framed her for the charge. But the arrest and subsequent bail she offered through the family charity gave her the opening to exact some gratitude in the form of a secret safe deposit box in Maggie's name. The authorities would turn the world over looking for the missing money. But one place they'd never look for it was in a random safe deposit box under the name of a homeless addict.

Maggie probably never knew what was in the box, if she even knew of its existence. She'd never get the chance anyway. She met her end in the desert, unaware that her life was more valuable than her name because it gave Karen the chance to escape forever. I wondered how much Arturo knew. Perhaps he was in on the plan all along, only to be betrayed by his wife at the eleventh hour. Only Julie could answer that now.

Julie probably thought that entire chapter of her life was safely behind her. But thirty years later, under financial pressure from an ill-advised expansion of her business, she had to revisit it. There was "free" money just sitting there. It was the answer to all her problems. All she had to do was get the owner of the box, Maggie, to be legally declared dead, then have Maggie's brother James Fitch claim his sister's property. But one part of the plan with Lois didn't make sense.

"Once Fitch learned about the money in his sister's name, why would he need you guys?" I asked.

Mr. Hearns shook his head sadly.

"I told her over and over to walk away. This was a bad deal."

Fitch's barroom claim that he was cheated out of a fortune actually had validity. Julie and Lois must have spun a story about the money and conveniently left out how much actually was in the account. He barely got a finder's fee on what should have been all his.

"He wasn't happy," said Hearns.

"So Fitch found out what they were up to."

"He was an idiot but he was no dummy. He started to make noise. That's when Lo asked me for help."

Hearns soon found himself embroiled in the whole affair. I probed for what he knew about the original source of the money, but it didn't sound like he was aware of Julie's past. He just knew the money didn't come from legitimate means.

Fitch started doing his own investigating in Phoenix and all the secrets began to trickle out. I assumed that Fitch's snooping around had alerted Arturo to what his ex-wife was up to. Now her secret was fully exposed to all the participants.

"What happened the day Lois was killed?"

"She and Fitch were supposed to meet at Julie's house. I told Lo that I would go with her, you know, to try to help out. This Fitch guy was pissed off. He didn't seem all there, either. Supposedly they all were going to work out a deal. She told me not to come along." His words fell flat. It was hard, even after the fact, to believe a deal could be worked out with anything less than one hundred percent of the money going to Fitch. "And that was it. The last I spoke to her."

He jiggled his can to calculate if it was too much to drain in a single pull.

"The cops say Fitch killed her," Hearns said.

"It looks that way."

"Nah," he shook his head. "That old hag killed her."

He stared into his beer for some support but didn't find any there.

"Whatever happened to the money?" I asked casually, after a few moments of silence. I wanted to see how honest he was being with me.

"Lo got some, Fitch got less, that witch got the rest," he replied. "Lo tried to give me some. Maybe ten grand, I don't know. I never counted it. Kept it in a bag in the freezer," he said, pointing to the garage fridge, which served as his beer cooler. "You know that night you came out here, I took the money and burned it. Got an old hubcap, a little gasoline…gone."

His eyes were getting glassy.

"Dirty money," he whispered.

I declined the offer for another beer. He again had that look of a man determined to get drunk and he didn't need my help doing it. I left him alone in his garage with his tools and tall boys and didn't say goodbye.

A LONELY, COLORLESS RAIN

The easy part was guessing where the body was buried. The difficult task was getting it out of the ground.

The old hunting retreats were built so close together that even the smallest of machinery couldn't fit between the buildings. Also, the street wasn't wide enough to drive a crane up to lift an excavator over the house. And access from the back was impossible without an amphibious landing unit to navigate the mountain run-off channel filled with roiling water. The only way to dig the old librarian's body out of the ground was with some spit on the hands and a couple of jackhammers and shovels.

I sat at the little café and nursed a coffee at the counter. The place was unusually empty given the cold, drizzly rain outside. It seemed like the entire neighborhood was up the road watching the proceedings at Julie St. Jean's old house.

The old man behind the counter barely acknowledged my presence, outside of a wordless refill of my mug. I assumed he was annoyed at the commotion I'd unleashed on his peaceful community and perhaps even the disruption to his regular business on a quiet Wednesday morning.

The Sierra Madre police weren't exactly discreet when announcing their plans to look for Julie St. Jean's body. The thirty-year-old mystery had become a bit of a local hullaballoo. I could hear the unmistakable whir of news helicopters overhead. Their counterparts on the ground were directed by the police to stay at the bottom of the hill, which meant they were lined up in the few parking spots in front of the old man's shop. With each broadcast back to the studio, the camera lights illuminated the coffee shop in a cold glare, further angering an already fully annoyed man.

"Couldn't leave well enough alone," he muttered. "It's a goddamn circus. And a goddamn shame. That poor woman doesn't deserve any of this."

"What if it means proving she was murdered?" I asked, despite my instinct to stay quiet.

"So what if she was?"

"We could finally find her killer," I said.

"And then?"

"Find justice."

He didn't seem to see the value in that.

"And who is that going to help?" he challenged.

"Well, it will give closure to the whole thing."

"No one needs nothing closed."

I finally got what he was saying. Not everything has to be tied up with a nice ribbon. Everything doesn't have to be neat and tidy, especially when factoring in the cost.

"I'm sorry," I said.

I left the shop and zipped up my coat as I slid between the news crews. I headed up the road to where all the excitement was, but halfway there I banked to the right and worked my way between two houses separated by a rocky outcropping. The stone was slick with moss and difficult to climb. I scrambled up the hillside a bit farther and found a place to wait under an old oak.

There was one thing I'd heard Julie say that I couldn't reconcile. In the heated discussion with Arturo when she revealed she never loved him, she very clearly stated that there was only one person she had loved. For Rebecca's sake, I hoped it was her but needed to acknowledge that simply couldn't be true. Julie had had too many opportunities to show it and failed with each one. Lois seemed unlikely despite the sordid affair. Hearns more or less confirmed that the night I visited him in the garage, when he told me that Lois knew she was being used. And if it wasn't Arturo, that left only one person.

Down across the way, large tents glowed bright white in the otherwise dreary gray day. The pangs of jackhammers echoed throughout the ravine as they worked on the concrete slab underneath the librarian's house.

I waited out of sight near the area where I'd first spotted Julie from the back of the police car. If there was a chance she'd come it would likely be to this place. I knew I might have to wait a long time.

The rain was lighter under the oak canopy but the drops making it through were big. My raincoat started to fail after about an hour. Water first soaked through on my shoulders and then straight down my spine. I tried not to move because that only reminded me just how cold it felt to be in wet clothes. I also tried not to move because I didn't want to be spotted.

I finally saw movement up on the ridge and stepped deeper into the brush. After a few minutes of nothing happening, I assumed my eyes were playing tricks on me. But then I saw the figure again, moving down one of the narrow cuts in the hillside. It dipped in and out of the darkened boulders perched on each side of the path and eventually came down to my level. I waited until the figure was within several feet before stepping out from my concealed spot.

"I always picked you for the sentimental type," I said.

Julie or Karen or whatever she should be called pulled up short. She kept her hands in her pockets and subtly glanced around. I made a more deliberate scan of the area.

"Just me," I answered to the first question she wanted to ask. "And no, I don't think anyone would hear a gunshot with all that racket down there," I answered to her second unstated question.

"What do you want?"

"I'm not really sure," I said. "Maybe for you to admit you're a horrible person?"

"Would that make it better?"

"Probably not, but it might help some."

"You don't get it. Never have."

"Trust me, I get it. You're a fraud. You've always been one. You cheated people out of their money, then cheated the guy you did the cheating with. All that executive coaching was just another scam, only legal this time."

Julie wasn't up for a lecture.

"Does it make you feel better to highlight all of my flaws?"

"Will it make you feel better if we make this about me and not you?" I countered, and then thought of her greatest con. "You never even showed at the hospital, Julie."

"I couldn't go!" she shouted.

It was the first time I'd seen her display so much emotion.

"Keep telling yourself that. I'm sure if there'd been something in it for you, you'd have found a way to make it work. You know until the very last minute she believed someone actually cared about her?"

I remembered those final moments in the prep room. I remembered Rebecca's hand in mine and her staring at the door hoping someone would walk through it. No one did.

"She went over alone but believed there was someone by her side," I said. "That's a cruel trick."

She looked at me and took a half-step back. It could have been a move by someone about to flee. Or, it was just to get a little more distance between us to make the shot easier.

"I lied before," I told her. "I'm not alone up here. You're not getting out, even if you add me to the list of people you've killed."

"You always thought you were so smart," she said, shaking her head to signal how dumb she thought I was. "I only took one person's life."

"Just one?" I mocked.

"And it wasn't my idea," she whispered.

I followed Julie's glance down to the white tents and the bevy of activity around them. She seemed to get lost in gazing at them, as at clouds.

"She asked me to kill her."

"You're going to try to blame a dead woman, now?"

All along I anticipated another Julie yarn—obfuscation came so naturally to her that I never expected anything truthful to come out of her mouth—but this had a different tone.

"She knew who I was," she started.

"How?"

"Because I told her. One week after renting out the room, we were up late talking and I just dumped everything on her. It all came out in one long, babbling mess. Who I was, what I had done, the trouble I was in. Julie was that kind of person—you just had to tell her everything. There was no judgment. She just listened. I don't think we ever spoke about it again." After a moment passed, she added, "I fell in love with her at that moment."

Julie caught a glimpse of my reaction.

"You smug-faced son of a bitch," she hissed.

"Don't stop," I told her. "I want to hear the rest."

She claimed it was the librarian's idea to take her identity.

"She worked everything out—the driver's license, access to the bank account, and the story she would tell everyone. She spent a few weeks dropping hints around the neighborhood about how much she missed home, how she wanted to retire and move back to Florida."

"And why would she do all that, Julie?"

"Because she was sick," her voice faltered. "Really sick."

I barely caught the clarification over the sounds from down below. Her voice was nearly a whisper.

"She quit her job before it became obvious to everyone. And then we just went home. I didn't really understand it, or, it wasn't real until it was over." Julie started to cry. Through tears, she said, "I don't care if you don't believe any of this. I loved the woman. She gave me her life."

I didn't want to believe what felt like the truth.

"What do you mean by 'until it was over'?"

Julie hesitated. Either she lacked the details of the narrative or she didn't want to divulge them. I waited for her to collect herself. She eventually described the precipitous decline after the real Julie was diagnosed and refused treatment.

"I told her to see someone, to get some help, but I guess she knew it was hopeless. And who was I to tell her what to do? I had never done that before and I wasn't about to start. She wouldn't have listened. Julie didn't see anything heroic in fighting it."

I recalled a similar statement from Rebecca.

"How did she die?"

"Pills," she answered, but provided no more details around how it went down, just an observation seared into her memory that felt as real to her today as it was on that night. "You should have heard the breathing," she shuddered. "I couldn't do it."

"Do what?" I asked.

"Stop it."

I processed her words. I looked across the way at the white orbs glowing brighter in the darkening day. If Julie's body was down there as everyone thought, the question still to be answered was: How did it get there? Julie would have needed help dragging it down the steps, digging a hole in the glacial bedrock, pouring a concrete slab over it, and— from the way she described the final minutes of the librarian's life—she would have needed help snuffing out her final breaths.

"Who helped you?" I asked, even though I already knew the answer.

"Please, can we not do this?"

"If he's in on it, people are going to need to know."

"Can't we just leave the poor man alone," she begged, using the same language he had used when describing his old friend. "He doesn't need to be dragged back in after all these years."

I looked down at the old coffee shop. If the truth was to come out, I didn't know how he could be spared.

But Julie had a way.

"I'll take the blame," she said. "He doesn't need to be brought back into this after what he did for me."

"Julie, if this is all true, then why did you say you killed her?"

"Because I let her do it. None of this should have ever happened."

She started to sound like the Julie I knew in one of her training sessions, when she dropped pearls of wisdom on us—composed, at peace, and in charge. She steeled herself and stared down at the white tents where what seemed like the entire Sierra Madre police forced milled about in rain slickers.

"I guess this is it," she said. "You said it was a dirty trick that I pulled on Rebecca..." her voice drifted. "Chuck, I just couldn't watch that happen to someone again."

It didn't absolve her, but I couldn't condemn her, either.

Julie took a hesitant step down the hill, then looked back.

"Will you walk down with me?" she asked.

I found myself reaching out and taking her hand. We only made it a few feet of the way.

The sound of the blast was instantaneous but felt like it came several seconds later. Julie fell forward, her grip tightening as she collapsed. I looked down at her body, which resembled more of a crumpled mess in the mud than the person who just moments ago had gestured for me to hold her hand. It took me a moment to realize that she still held it.

I frantically scanned the woods and caught movement as someone emerged from a clump of pines. It was the old man from the coffee shop. He carried a long gun.

I freed myself from Julie's grip and quickly searched her pockets. The only thing I came out with was a crimson-stained hand. She had come unarmed.

And now, so was I.

RUN-OFF

Down the hill, the old man slowly worked his way up toward me. The only path to escape was to move farther away from the road, the very place where I might find some form of rescue.

I ran as hard as I could on the spongy bed of pine needles, slipping a few times but gradually able to put some distance between me and the old man. I followed alongside the concrete run-off channel, a deep gouge in the hillside that carried rainwater down into the valley. Under the gray, roiling surface, massive rocks jostled in the fury and over the deafening roar came a sickening sound when two boulders smashed together.

There was a rusty footbridge over the run-off channel up ahead. I ran across it and nearly slid over the edge when my shoes gave way on the slick surface. Looking down, it felt like the water was dangerously close to sweeping the entire bridge away.

I crawled the rest of the way and then continued up the hill on the opposite side of the channel. Twice I looked back and saw no sign of the old man. But I did see a figure up ahead walking in the same direction I was headed.

"Help!" I shouted.

The figure didn't hear me over the rush of water in the channel next to us. I closed the gap and then called out again.

"Help me!"

This time he stopped and turned around.

It was Detective Fortin.

I ran toward him, despite the unanswered questions that should have led me to do the opposite. Even he was a bit surprised by what I was doing. But I ran toward him simply because he wasn't the man with the gun behind me.

Once I reached an arm's-length distance, Detective Fortin pulled out a gun of his own. I blinked away the rain and stared at it hanging by his side.

"Oh, no," I said out loud as I realized I was running from the wrong man with the gun.

"Yeah," he confirmed almost reluctantly.

I processed what it meant that he'd been in Los Angeles since his "disappearance" and realized that it went further than that.

"You've been in LA the whole time," I said.

Detective Fortin was there from the start, which meant he was involved from the very beginning.

Everything started to take on some semblance of

order again. The discrepancy of a homeless addict getting arrested on a felony intent-to-distribute drug charge made sense when you understood that the arresting officer had ulterior motives. It was a trumped-up charge. It also helped explain how that same officer overlooked the fact that the woman who posted her bail was under investigation for fraud. Poor detective skills had nothing to do with him looking the other way. He did it on purpose because it was all part of the plan he had with Karen Arturo. They now had the leverage to get Maggie to do whatever they asked, including opening an account in which to hide money from the authorities.

One detail I didn't understand was why the money sat for so long. The plan was clearly hatched between Detective Fortin and Karen. They subsequently murdered Maggie and staged it to frame Karen's husband. With Phil Arturo arrested for her own murder, she was free to escape with the money. Instead, she fled to Los Angeles penniless and reinvented herself as a consultant guru. And three decades later, under extreme financial pressures, she finally set in motion the process to obtain the money.

Something Julie said the night she tried to collect the millions in my office gave me an answer. She'd made a comment about doing some bad things but then it got far worse than she'd ever imagined. Perhaps killing Maggie was never part of the plan.

"She didn't kill any of them," I said, realizing that Julie was telling the truth before she was shot.

Detective Fortin looked away.

"None of them?"

"They were all crooks," he tried to justify.

I assumed Detective Fortin learned of Karen's where-abouts when Fitch went snooping around Arizona in search of the money. He likely used Fitch in the same fashion that Julie and Lois had done. Perhaps he even convinced Fitch to dispose of Lois and with that deed completed, he then disposed of Fitch and tried to lay it on the woman who had double-crossed him so many years back. But one thing kept him from getting the money—it was riding along in the back of my trunk.

My mind raced back to the night Arturo was shot. "Again" took on greater meaning. He couldn't believe the two people who'd tried to destroy him three decades ago were doing it again. And they had an accomplice. Lying there on the floor among construction detritus, he made the connection to the man who shot him and the calls made to Arizona on my cell phone. He died believing I had set him up. And that was something I could never undo.

"Arturo thought I was in on it," I said.

"He was a sap, too," Detective Fortin replied.

The qualifier could reference many people. Maybe we were all saps in his view. But there was something in his tone that made me wonder if the events from three decades ago went beyond money.

"She betrayed you, too?" I asked.

This time he didn't have a quick answer. He had one more task to take care of.

With Julie dead, there was no one left who could

tie him to any of it. He was free to spend his millions in retirement without fear of anything or anyone coming back to implicate him. But then I had to stumble upon him in the woods. And now one more person with the knowledge to hurt him had to be removed.

We both scanned the area and came to the same conclusion but with different interpretations—no help was coming.

"Why did you even get involved?" he asked.

"I don't know," I said.

Detective Fortin opened his coat and pulled his shirttail out from his waistline. I watched him methodically wipe down the gun and then point it at me again, but this time ensuring he left no fingerprints on it.

"Jump," he said.

"What?" I asked, even though I understood what he intended to do.

I looked down at the roiling water. There was no swimming out of that cauldron.

"I'm sorry," he said.

"Detective—"

"I'm sorry," he repeated.

"I'm not going to jump," I heard myself saying. "You'll have to shoot me."

He stared at me, and I thought I was getting through to him.

But then he looked away. My eyes widened.

The roar of a gun boomed in my ear and I felt warm, stinging pain up and down my leg. I stumbled and fell to one knee. Detective Fortin tumbled backward, clutching his side as he tried to balance on the slick slope. He caught hold of my jacket with his free hand and pulled me toward him and the run-off channel edge. His feet went up and over the side, and I almost went with him. My face ground into the mud as I scratched at anything to keep from slipping in.

A pair of hands tugged at my hurt leg and slowed my descent. I steadied myself at the edge and looked down at Detective Fortin dangling over the water. He had one hand gripping my jacket and the other gripping the channel's concrete wall.

I watched Detective Fortin close his eyes like he was taking a nap in a hammock on a warm day. Then he eased his grip on the wall. My jacket tore away and his body fell into the gray wash and was whisked downhill faster than I thought possible. It rolled and tumbled over the boulder bottom before getting hung up. As I watched, transfixed, it became another immovable object that couldn't stop the rush of mountain water in the channel intent on finding its final resting place at the bottom of the hill.

CHARTREUSE

For the second time that day, modern machinery failed authorities. The hillside around the run-off channel was inaccessible to cranes and the treetops obstructed access from the helicopters above. So the task of removing Detective Fortin's body from the wash fell on the Fire & Rescue team, which ended up performing a high-wire act of sorts, in which one unlucky member was lowered into the morass to secure a rope around the body so it could be lifted out.

Sierra Madre suddenly had three active crime scenes. A single murder threatened to overwhelm the small police force; three sent it into full-blown disarray. But in the immediate aftermath, it was surprisingly serene.

I rose up out of the mud and inspected the back of my leg, which was riddled with shotgun pellets. They stung mightily, but I gladly took the pain in exchange for my life.

The old man from the coffee shop broke the shotgun barrel into safety formation.

"Can you walk?" he asked.

I nodded.

"I'll stay here while you go get help."

I limped my way down the hill and returned some time later with a skeptical junior officer in tow. The old man was in the same position as when I'd left him.

"What's going on, Pete?" the officer asked the old man.

It was the first time I'd heard the name of the man who saved my life.

"There's a body down there," he said, gesturing toward the run-off channel. "I shot him. There's another down the hill a ways. The dead man shot her."

The young officer looked into the channel and spotted the body and then looked around for Julie's body, but it wasn't visible from our position. By the time he turned back, Pete had the shotgun held out for him to take.

"Better use a handkerchief," Pete suggested, and even offered his own after the officer's pockets came up empty. "We'll also need to talk about the body you all are digging up down there. I know a little something about that."

That's how it went. Pete told them everything, including the incriminating confession that he physically ended the old librarian's life and helped bury the body underneath the house. I also went the full-disclosure route and divulged every last bit of information I had about Detective Fortin and the events in Arizona from thirty years ago.

It all felt a little overwhelming for the Sierra Madre police so they were more than willing to let their big sister to the west help out. Los Angeles forensics eventually matched the bullets that killed Fitch, Arturo, and Julie/Karen to the gun they pulled out of the water with Detective Fortin's body. Pete was cleared of any wrongdoing as it related to the detective's death, his actions justified by the circumstances and corroborated by the only witness at the scene. That left one more "murder"—the one involving the body buried under the old hunting lodge.

It was clear from the outset that the Sierra Madre police department had little interest in pursuing a charge against Pete. It was as if they were channeling Pete's own plea to leave well enough alone. But he had made the confession and did so in the presence of quite a few people, including me. The police didn't want to pursue it but they couldn't ignore it, either.

Their way out came three weeks later while searching the safe deposit box at the Pasadena bank that Julie had visited hours after Lois's murder. It contained an unopened letter postmarked 1985. In it, the real Julie St. Jean outlined the entire scheme to end her life. It was insurance in case the truth came out, as it had done some thirty years later.

I now understood the frantic visit to the bank. Julie needed to store the letter in a safe place in case she was ever caught. In the end, it didn't save her neck but it did save Pete's. The letter was all a reluctant police force needed to officially close the case with no charges levied. If pressed, they would ignore Pete's confession and place the blame on a dead woman. For once, I was grateful for a police force that didn't follow the rules.

Despite all the cases being wrapped up, the casualties continued to mount, though none as dire as the five dead—six, if you counted Maggie Fitch. Among the casualties was a professional career that never should have risen as high as it did and was already teetering on collapse.

My position as head of the group was tenuous from the start. Pat Faber never wanted me to have the role and probably looked for any reason to snatch it away. I gave him more than he needed.

While terminations were an extended ordeal, demotions were swift. I knew the hammer was going to fall but the form in which it would come was a mystery. The one thing I did know—it wouldn't be straightforward. The first clue came in a predawn touch-base with Pat.

"How do we know we're connecting the dots?" he asked me.

"Elaborate, if you could," I requested, even though I knew this was the opening he sought.

"The connections between the work you're doing, the work from the Wellness group, and the work Benefits is leading."

As the head of all three of those groups, Pat was

supposed to be the person "connecting the dots." But I knew enough not to point that out, because he clearly had an agenda to deliver.

"Feels like there's a gap," he said.

And gaps always needed to be filled, I concluded.

A new role was created above me to address Pat's nonexistent problem; then Paul Darbin was asked to fill it. That's how we tacitly switched positions, and the man whom I lorded over became my boss.

Badger's contract was the next casualty.

With Paul finally in charge of the group and the purse strings that kept it running, he decided that Badger and his consistently stellar work, trustworthiness, and rock-bottom hourly rate were just too good a bargain to keep under contract with our firm. He was soon replaced by an unscrupulous investigator with a nicer suit and a college-level vocabulary who charged twenty times Badger's rate for a fraction of the work but at least wouldn't offend Native American colleagues with culturally insensitive remarks about "wigwams."

With what I assumed was his only income pipeline sealed off, I felt a need to put Badger right. For once, I wished he wasn't so honest. The money delivered on the night Arturo was shot, which was eventually recovered from Detective Fortin's car, had every last dollar accounted for.

"Couldn't a few hundred K have gotten 'lost' in all this?" I asked him, as I wrote out a hefty check for his services from the last few weeks.

"No can do, chief," he answered, bringing the check

up to his nose for a deep inhalation. "I couldn't afford to lose your respect."

And I couldn't afford for him to keep it. The list of home renovations would sit for another year until the next bonus cycle, as grim a prospect as that was becoming.

The thought that Paul was now the sole arbiter of my earnings made me shudder. I wasn't exactly the fairest manager when I had the role as head of the department, and now that our positions were switched, I braced for retribution that would be fast and deep.

His first order of business was to ink ColorNalysis to a very generous contract to lead employee engagement. The second was to put me in charge of making them a success.

And so I was back in the workshop business, leading endless sessions featuring new gimmicks that tried to solve old problems. Bronson never worked on the programs directly. The guru talked strategy with his disciple, Paul, but the actual work fell on me and the matronly woman he had working for him.

"Let's have Chuck and Ethel iron out the details," he said, smiling.

One gem of an idea was to physically wear the color representing the personality you needed to develop. That way you projected an image of strength where you actually had weakness. All it did was set people back several hundred bucks on refreshed wardrobes. And it sentenced me to a month of wearing so much yellow that by the end of it I actually felt jaundiced.

"Hey, buttercup," Bronson joked one day in the hall. "You should choose a personality that comes with a more appealing color."

"Where's yours?" I challenged, but he laughed it off as a foolish question not worth addressing.

"You'll never get it, Chuck," he said.

"Julie said that to me once. It must be in the consultant handbook."

"Why can't you see we're doing good work here?" he asked. "We're making progress."

"Hamsters think they're making progress, too."

"Not *think*," he corrected. "*Believe*. That's what you'll never understand."

I finally got it a few weeks later during another engagement workshop. The young mom who had participated in the survey results, the one who foolishly shared her true feelings to a group of people who didn't care, was at it again in front of the same set of managers. She looked to still be on the journey toward her "pre-baby weight" and she still got nervous when speaking in front of others, but there was something different this time. There was certitude in the way she talked about how much better things had gotten. And it all had to do with the workshop I led.

"Thank you," her voice quavered, her splotchy cheeks an almost perfect match to the shade of salmon she'd been wearing for the last few months. "I'm a different person now."

She really believed this nonsense. And trying to disabuse her of it felt like an unnecessarily cruel act. Also, she wasn't the only one clinging to an irrational belief.

For six months, out of some silly fear that removing her belongings would somehow erase her memory, I delayed cleaning out the room where Rebecca had stayed. That sort of decision wasn't exactly prudent when paying an exorbitant amount per square foot on a room that I would never use. But as a divorced man with no kids and no prospects for any, the small bedroom had little value to me so I just left it for another day.

About the Author

Adam Walker Phillips is the author of two previous novels, *The Silent Second* and *The Perpetual Summer.* An executive at a global financial services company, he has endured countless PowerPoint decks, offsite visioning sessions, synergies, and synergistically minded cross-functional teams, all in service of telling the stories of Chuck Restic, an HR man–turned–moonlighting detective. Phillips lives in the Eagle Rock neighborhood of Los Angeles with his wife and children.